"Evan, there's no shame in seeking help." Rose's voice was soft.

And her mouth was close to him. He could feel her breath on his hair.

"I have what I need. Believe me, I'm working through it." He looked at her then. "Stop being a doctor."

She stared into his eyes. Her hands still held his and they still shook. The rest of his body he held rigidly in check.

"I'll stop being a doctor," she said, raising a hand and running it along the contours of his jaw. "But I'm still your friend."

With that she stood. Evan moved back and she passed him to go to the door.

"Think you can get some sleep now?" she asked.

He was suddenly tired. "I think so."

"Good night then."

"Good night, Rose."

Neither of them mo~~ved~~. F~~or a~~ charged moment they stared at each ~~other~~ was seeing her for t~~he~~ known her all of hi~~s~~

D0831334

SHIRLEY HAILSTOCK

began her writing life as a lover of reading. She liked nothing better than to find a corner in the library and get lost in a book, exploring new worlds or visiting places she never expected to see. As an author, she has not only visited those places, but she can be the heroine of her own stories.

A past president of Romance Writers of America, Shirley holds a bestselling romance award from Waldenbooks and a Career Achievement Award from *Romantic Times BOOKreviews*. She is the recipient of the Emma Merritt Award for service to RWA and the Lifetime Achievement Award from the New York City Chapter. Contact Shirley at shailstock@aol.com or visit her Web site at www.geocities.com/shailstock.

SHIRLEY HAILSTOCK

My Lover, My Friend

KIMANI
ROMANCE

To Marion, the boy next door.

Acknowledgments

Thanks go to my friend and fellow author Kelly McClymer.
Kelly, a lifelong resident of Maine, was invaluable in helping me
with the setting and the lighthouse information for this book. She took
photographs of the land and sea and mailed them to me along with a
book so I could "hear" the sound of the Maine voice. Plus she answered
pages of questions. Thank you is too small a phrase to acknowledge
her help. If there are any errors, they are, of course, mine.

 KIMANI PRESS™

RECYCLED PAPER · RECYCLED PAPER

ISBN-13: 978-1-58314-787-0
ISBN-10:   1-58314-787-X

MY LOVER, MY FRIEND

www.kimanipress.com

Printed in U.S.A.

Dear Reader,

Many of us know the expression "boy next door," but how many of us actually lived next door to a good-looking boy who grew into a gorgeous man? I did, and he was the inspiration for *My Lover, My Friend*. I also love lighthouses and craggy coastlines where the wind and surf pound against the rocks. So setting my book around a lighthouse in Maine was a no-brainer.

The hero, Evan Harper, jogged into my mind over the noise of that pounding surf. Though he's missing the dimples of my real-life boy next door, he has a winning smile and a good heart. And he's trying to avoid an emotional problem that Rose, the local doctor and his childhood friend, would help him work out.

I hope you enjoy your time with Rose and Evan, and that you've found your own boy next door, no matter whose door he was next to.

Sincerely yours,

Shirley Hailstock

Chapter 1

Black water swirled below the bridge. Evan Harper couldn't see it. The night was black. Everything around him was black. Low angry clouds rumbled and rolled about the heavens, speaking to him in a tongue he didn't understand. Or one he didn't want to understand.

The bridge, a metal span over the Lighthouse River, connected Allison Avenue South to its sister on the north. Painted black years ago, in daylight chipped rust stains were changing the hue to an orange-red. Trees and bushes along the shoreline were indistinct in the dark, blending in with the inky surroundings and melting the entire scene into nothing.

Evan gripped the small silver baby rattle in his big hand. A tear fell on it and he wiped it away with his thumb. The rattle was smaller than his index finger, shaped like a bone, a perfect fit for Gabe to hold. Other than Evan's fingers pulling the child up and letting him jump like a toy puppet, the rattle was the only thing his three-month-old hands could hold.

He would never hold it again.

Squeezing his eyes shut and swallowing the lump in his throat, Evan tried to block the images that formed in his head, torturing him. The flash of flames tearing through wood and siding, crackling as it ate away the structure, and the restraining hold of strong arms keeping him back as he struggled to get to the burning house.

Tears seeped from the corners of his eyes and rolled unchecked down his face. There was nothing he could have done, except die with him. There was no way to stop the flames, the smoke or the tiny voice that cried for help inside his head.

Evan opened his eyes. Using the back of his hands, he wiped the tears away and took several deep breaths.

Put it behind you, people had told him. Evan almost laughed at the thought. How do you put something like that behind you? How do you forget a child? He didn't understand men who left their children, walked away from the precious gift of life as if the child didn't matter and never looked back. Didn't they know how lucky they were? How could they stare into an innocent face that only asked to be loved and turn away? How could they endure the pain?

Evan pulled his jacket closer around him. Hunching his aching shoulders, he pushed his hands into his pockets, trying to hold the anguish that knifed through his insides. It always came like this, fresh, raw, hot and unexpected. He'd think he had conquered it, that his life was getting on track, that the platitudes people told him about being able to live with it were true, that he was finally, after two years, going to be all right. Then without warning the fire would came back; the confusion, fire trucks, men in yellow and black with big boots traipsing about and the bands holding him in place. The rope of hands keeping him still when all he wanted to do was get to Gabe. He'd wake up bathed in sweat, the covers ripped from the bed as if he'd been fighting them, or find himself sitting in his office staring through the window with no recollection of what he was doing.

Gripping the cold metal struts of the bridge,

Evan stepped back, elongating his body like an athlete stretching muscles in preparation to run. He jogged daily. He'd tried to run, tried to outrun the pain, the incessant visions, but nothing helped.

So he'd come back here. Back to Lighthouse, Maine, where life was slower than it was in D.C. Where there were no memories of Gabe. Evan would give himself some time, the way his doctor suggested. Maybe he'd go to the old lighthouse and help paint the outside. They were always looking for volunteers. His Boy Scout troop had worked on it. Painting was mindless and that's exactly what he needed. He didn't need people or want them around. The lighthouse didn't speak, didn't offer condolences, didn't look at him with sad, pitiful eyes.

A car swung onto the bridge as the first drops of rain plopped against the metal railing. Evan looked around. Headlights shone in his eyes. He squinted, his hand holding the rattle came up quickly as he shaded his eyes. The mixture of salt and high-beamed illumination clashed in a shock of pain. The car passed him, but slowed to a stop several feet behind his. He slipped the toy into his pocket, still concentrating on the water. He wanted no company. His whole being was absorbed in grief and he didn't want to explain anything, even to a stranger.

Footsteps clicked on the concrete ground as they came toward him. They were tentative and female. He heard the heels of her shoes as she moved.

"Evan?"

It was almost a whisper. He turned. A woman stood a few feet away. It was too dark to see her face. She wore a long dress or skirt with a jacket. And high heels. There was something familiar about her.

"Evan, is that you?" She took another step forward but appeared ready to run back to her car if he turned out to be someone else.

"Who is it?" he asked.

"Evan," she cried and ran, arms outstretched, toward him. He hadn't had time to process who she was before her body slammed into his. Her arms climbed around his neck in a tight hug. It had been a long time since he'd held a woman. Without volition his arms surrounded her thin body and he held her lightly. She felt good. Too good for someone he didn't know. Emotions he'd relegated behind a high-security fence in his heart found an opening and raced through it.

"When did you get back?" She spoke against his ear. Her voice was breathy and did funny things to the hair on his neck.

He pressed himself against her, closing his eyes at the heat she generated, burying his head in her neck and inhaling her. There was a sweet perfume on her skin, a fragrant scent on her hair that mingled with traces of soap or shampoo. He was amazed he could identify each of the scents separately. Evan knew it was wrong to feel like this, to hold this stranger and examine personal things about her, but she was here and he needed someone. He needed to hold someone close.

Would she understand that when he pushed her away? How long had he been holding her? He didn't want to let go, not for another minute. He loosened his arms but kept her aligned with him. His hands ran over her back. Finally, she pulled back. Her hair slipped over her shoulder and he could see her face.

"Rose?"

"You sound surprised. Who did you think I was?" she asked.

In light of how Evan was holding her, he hesitated a moment before answering. "Of course I knew it was you. I didn't expect you to be so…beautiful." Evan wasn't kidding when he said that. He hadn't seen Rosamund Albright in nine years and she was gorgeous even in this weak light. The two had been the best of friends when he lived in Lighthouse, Maine. But he'd gone away to college and law school and eventually settled in D.C. working as a speechwriter for Senator Katherine DeLong of Illinois.

"That's probably not the truth, but it's a good answer."

"You haven't changed a bit." He smiled. Evan released her, reluctantly, he noted, and looked back at the distance over the bridge. He hadn't totally regained control of himself and he didn't want Rose to notice. She'd always known when something was wrong with him. Rose had been like a sister to him. Yet tonight, holding her in his arms, he'd had no brotherly thoughts. Initially, she was just another human being, someone to hold close while emotions warred inside him. But somewhere that had changed and she became a soft, sweet-smelling and sexually appealing woman.

"We all change, Evan." She leaned against the bridge's metal structure next to him, but not close enough to touch. "What are you doing out here?" she asked.

"I just got back. When I turned onto the bridge I thought I'd stop and survey the land."

"You mean the dark," she corrected. "You can barely see a thing tonight. But I can hear you. And you talk funny."

"I don't talk funny."

She laughed. "You've been gone a long time. You sound more like a Washington politician than the Maine boy next door."

"Just scratch me," he said. "I'm sure you'll find the lighthouse circulating in my blood."

"It's so good to see you again." She hugged him a second time but pushed back quickly. "It's raining." She opened her hand and as if on cue a raindrop plopped directly in her palm, followed by more. The misty air turned to misty rain. Evan took her hand, combining the moisture with his own. "Let's get out of here. I remember how vicious the weather can turn."

He walked her to her car. "Are you staying at your old house?" Rose asked.

He nodded. "My parents will be in Egypt for a while. I had cleaned and aired it a week ago. And if I know Mrs. Reed she'll have stocked the refrigerator."

"I have a casserole waiting."

"Sounds delicious." Evan raised an eyebrow.

"Have you eaten?"

"I wasn't fishing for an invitation."

"I know."

"It's my first night back. I think I'll just go on and see what the house looks like."

"You have to eat."

"I'll grab something on the way."

"Not here. The only restaurant in town closed at nine." She paused and looked at his car, which was hidden in the darkness. "Is someone waiting for you?"

"That's not it," he said.

"Good," she cut in before he could say anything more. "You know where I live."

With that, she pushed away from him and got into her car. Turning back to wave at him, she drove away. Evan strode to his SUV with a smile. He hadn't smiled in a long time and it felt good. Rose had always been bossy and she hadn't changed a bit. He found that comforting. At least something in his life was stable.

The rain was coming down steadily, washing away his bleak mood. Rose always could make him feel better. But she couldn't put all the pieces of his life back together again.

The last man on earth Rose expected to find on the Allison Avenue bridge was Evan Harper. They'd been best friends since she could remember. He'd looked good in the misty glow of her headlights, but under the bright fluorescence of her spacious kitchen, he was gorgeous. He always had been good looking but his eyes…something was different. They were tired looking, but she could see something in their depths that was wiser. His hair was shorter than it had been nine years ago, but that was due to changing styles. His face was clean-shaven and his smile showed even, white teeth. Strange, Rose thought. Why hadn't she ever noticed how broadly his clothes fit across his

shoulders or how long his legs were? He wore
boots with his jeans, but had abandoned a
matching jacket to the back of a chair. His white
shirt still looked freshly starched. It was opened
at the neck, and a triangle of delectable skin
peeked out. For an insane moment while he was
walking around the room, Rose wanted to touch
the dark brown skin with reddish undertones that
was exposed between the open collar. Suddenly
she knew what it was that was new in Evan—sex
appeal. Girls at school had always been after him.
He'd dated a lot, but this was the first time Rose
had felt the pull of his charm. She stopped that
train of thought. What was wrong with her? She
and Evan had never been anything more than very
good friends. Maybe it was that hug on the bridge,
she thought. He'd held her longer than he should
have and a flood of emotions she hadn't felt in a
year rushed over her like gurgling water over river
rocks.

"It's been a long time since I had a home-
cooked meal," Evan said as he finished eating. His
voice snapped Rose back to the present.

"It's that fast life you live," she told him.

He put his fork down then picked it up again.
He didn't eat anymore, only rat-a-tat-tated it on the
plate. Rose stood up, taking her plate to the sink,
giving herself time to become acquainted with the

thought that had just gone through her mind. Evan followed her. Rose took his dishes, leaving them in the sink. She'd clean them later. Carrying a tray with coffee cups, she bypassed the closed pocket doors of the dining room and led him into the great room. It was her favorite room in the house and where they'd once spent many hours engaged in adolescent activities.

Evan was a virtual celebrity in a town as small as Lighthouse. When word got around that he'd returned, people would be pounding at his door the way they had when he was the local hunk. Now he was a hunk returned. Rose set the tray on a low table and put her hand on her stomach to calm the butterflies.

"You always liked living fast."

He nodded. "I like it." He sat down, but stood up again almost immediately.

Rose observed his discomfort. Did she make him nervous? It had been years since they'd seen each other. And people did change. He'd gone to D.C. and worked in a fast-paced world where decisions affected millions. She'd become the town doctor dealing with anything that came her way.

Evan went to the unlit fireplace and sipped his coffee.

"You never know what's going to happen from

one day to the next. Most days you work on pure adrenaline."

"I like knowing what I'm going to do," Rose said.

"Since when?" He raised an eyebrow. "As I recall, you were going to go to med school and become a world-class surgeon. Travel the world performing miracles on a daily basis."

"I found out miracles are a little harder than I thought they'd be. And you can be a world class surgeon in a small town." She smiled. "I did half of it. I'm the local doctor here." Rose's life had changed in med school. It seemed that coming home was more important than the dream she'd once had. Closing her eyes, she pushed away the ghostly memories.

"I saw your license tag." Evan balanced his cup in his hands, then rolled it between them. Rose didn't need LOCAL DR written on the personalized tag to tell everyone around here what she did. She'd grown up in this town. She knew everyone and they all knew her.

"The tag was a present from Doc Kidd. When I returned after my residency and set up a practice, he presented it to me on my first day in the office."

"Doc Kidd is still practicing medicine? He must be older than dirt by now."

"He retires at the end of the year."

"And you'll be the only doctor in town."

"That's right," she said. The thought was scarier than it sounded. She'd had Doc Kidd to back her up since her return. When he retired she'd be responsible for the medical care of five hundred families. Lighthouse was a small town and most people wouldn't think there would be more than colds and ingrown toenails to treat. But they'd be wrong. A small-town doctor had to be ready for any and every kind of emergency. In her time here she'd done everything a small MASH unit would do on the perimeter of a war. Portland was seventy-five miles away and if anything arose she couldn't handle, she'd call for a Medivac. In the meantime, it was up to her to keep patients alive.

"Haven't you ever wanted to leave? To see what's happening in the world?" He said it as if she were wasting her life here.

"I've traveled and been around. I did my residency in Boston. But I like the quiet life here. I can't imagine living anywhere else." Rose slipped out of her shoes and curled her feet under her on the sofa. "Since you asked, I take it this will be a short visit for you? The big city calls."

"Three months," he said.

"That's a definite amount of time. What are you planning to do?"

"Play some golf, read, relax."

"What about Mrs. Harper? Didn't I hear that you got married?" Her voice sounded a little tight when she said that. She'd always felt a little angry that Evan hadn't invited her to his wedding. Although, from what she'd heard, he hadn't had a white-gown-and-tuxedo event, more like a skip over the county line and find a justice of the peace. She couldn't fault him. Her own marriage had been performed in much the same manner—quick, with only a few people as witnesses.

"It didn't work out. We divorced."

Rose was sure she'd seen a twinge of pain on his face when she asked the question. Was he still in love with his wife?

"What about you, no husband?"

"He died." Rose sipped her coffee. She wouldn't go into the details. Evan would learn them soon enough.

"I'm sorry. I didn't know," Evan said.

"It's all right. I've come to terms with it."

Rose didn't want to revisit her marriage, but thoughts came without volition. She'd met Brett Patterson in the park near Mass General. She'd come off a grueling thirteen-hour shift and was dead tired. He was a computer programmer who engineered his own software and consulted for several companies. Rose fell in love almost immediately when he sat down next to her. He was funny, sensitive and understanding. He could make her forget the long hours in the emergency room. When things started to get serious, he told her he had a heart condition. Still they were married. He collapsed and died several months later.

"How do you come to terms with death?" Evan asked. "I've never understood that."

Rose wondered if he was able to see into her head. His comment was so close to what she was feeling. It was eerie—as if their old connection had never faded.

He put his hand in his pocket and took it out again. She had seen him do that three times in the space of a minute. It was a nervous gesture he hadn't had when he lived in Lighthouse.

"You go on," she said. "You don't forget. You never forget, but you learn to live with the pain. Day by day it lessens. After a while you're ready to love again." Rose didn't know why she said that. For some strange reason, as she watched Evan clutching the coffee cup in his hands as if it was anchoring him to this place in the universe, she thought he needed to know. He said his marriage didn't work out, yet his actions indicated he remained in love with his wife. Divorce didn't mean you stopped loving someone.

"I'd better go." He cleared his throat and finally

set the cup on the table. Rose unfolded herself from her position and followed him to the door. At five feet, five inches, she felt short without her shoes, which she'd left behind. Evan stood like a giant over her. "Thank you for the meal."

"We'll have to do it again." Despite not having seen her old friend in years, she couldn't lie to herself. She wanted to see him again. His presence on the bridge had given her a jolt, especially when he'd held her close. Having him across her dinner table did crazy things to her stomach. Things she recognized but hadn't felt in a long time.

"We will," he said.

Rose knew he didn't mean it. She leaned against the wide front door, her cheek pressed against the painted wooden edge. Evan stepped down onto the walkway and went through the white picket fence. He raised his hand and waved good-night. She nodded and did the same. What a guy, she thought. And look what he'd grown into. He was head and shoulders above the pack—undoubtedly the most eligible bachelor in town.

And a man on the brink.

Rose's training hadn't only been to find physical problems in her patients but to read their symptoms too. Evan wasn't her patient, but she couldn't turn off her internal observer. Something was obviously wrong. He'd paced a lot, fiddled with his glass and fork, wrung his hands and acted as if he didn't know what to do next. The signs were there. Rest and relaxation were the best things for him. That was the real reason he was here.

She'd have to keep an eye on him. And that wouldn't be hard.

Rose waited a week before going to see Evan. She'd risen each morning and looked at Evan's house, knowing it was occupied, but there had been no sign of the owner in residence. Evan hadn't been anywhere in town, at least not anywhere that people could see him. She knew someone of his stature wouldn't go unnoticed. You'd think Mrs. Wormly, who was beyond retirement age, would be the town gossip, that she would have put the word out, but she used to work at the post office and took people's secrets to heart. If Evan asked her to keep quiet about anything, she'd go to her grave without divulging his secrets. That could be good, but to the doctor in town— namely her—Rose worried that he was ill and unable to call for help.

She didn't think this was the case, but it didn't hurt to check. Evan might be here to relax, but cloistering himself inside his house and avoiding everyone wasn't good for him.

Their houses sat side by side although they were vastly different in style and architecture. Hers was a Georgian with a huge foyer and an exquisitely carved staircase and woodwork. The three-story colonial with Cape Code attic windows had box hedges near the front and a white picket fence on the tree-lined street. Even though the house had central heating and air-conditioning, each room still has its own working fireplace.

Evan's house had been built in the early 1800s by a rich sea captain. Its style was Federalist, three stories with wide half-moon windows above the ornate front door, the second-floor landing and the attic-level center window. Surrounding the house was a newel-post fence. Five stone steps led up to the fence and walkway, then two additional steps to the porticoed front door. Rose had always loved his house. She liked looking out at the sea from the top floor or the balustraded parapet on top.

Rose stood shaded from the sun by a porch roof held up by two Corinthian columns. Ringing the doorbell, she waited for Evan to answer. It took a while. She rang it three times and was about to go across the street to Mrs. Reed and borrow a key or entice the older woman to come and open the door, when he appeared.

"Good morning," Evan said. "I'm sorry to keep

you waiting, but I wasn't expecting company." He looked as if she'd awakened him. He was wearing drawstring pajama bottoms and no shirt. The jolt that went through Rose at the sight of his naked chest and the hint of nothing beneath the thin pants was raw and electric. She nearly dropped the papers she was carrying. She was a doctor. She'd seen many chests before, but none put together like this one. His biceps were well defined and his pectorals looked as if they'd been carved by a student of Michelangelo. His stomach was lean and toned.

Clutching the papers in her hands against her own chest, Rose lowered her eyes, then quickly looked up again. Evan didn't seem to notice her reaction. Yet she remembered how his arms had enveloped her on the bridge. The hug had been almost desperate.

"Morning? It's well past noon." Rose swept by him, not giving him time to refuse her entry. "I see you're still jogging. Are you writing a book too?"

"Where'd you get an idea like that?"

"I'm a doctor. I carved it out of a medical book. Answer me."

"Of course I'm not writing a book." He passed her and went to the kitchen. Rose followed. Dropping her papers on the counter, she sat on a stool in front of it.

"You haven't been out of this house that I can tell. So I concluded that you must be writing a book."

Evan opened the refrigerator and took out a carton of orange juice. Holding it with both hands, he drank it straight from the container and pitched the carton toward the trash can. He missed. Rose picked it up and dropped it in the receptacle. She had to do *some*thing while she waited for an answer.

Evan got two glasses from the cabinet and a fresh carton of juice. Setting them on the counter, he poured and slid one to her.

"How many holes of golf have you played in the last week?" Rose asked.

"None."

"How many hours have you been asleep?"

"What is this?"

"It'll be an examination if that's necessary."

"Who have you been talking to?"

"I don't need to talk to anyone to see you're in a state of anxiety. You can't keep your hands still. You fidget." He stopped the action she was reciting. "What happened to you?"

"Nothing."

"Okay. What doctor sent you here?"

"None."

"Evan." She elongated his name and raised her eyebrows.

"I don't want to talk about it."

She sighed inwardly, relieved that he had sought medical help. "So you did see a doctor back in D.C."

He hooked his leg over a stool and sat down. His eyes were trained on the glass he held. It took a full minute for him to nod. In that time Rose studied him, trying to find out what it was about him that had her thoughts racing toward sexually entwined bodies. She'd never been that type of woman. At least not with a man she hadn't seen in almost a decade and hadn't really thought of as a sexual partner. But that was quickly changing.

"Are you on any medication?" she asked quietly.

"No."

"That's a start."

"No more questions," he said.

She had many questions, but she'd hold them. He was obviously not hurt or unable to call for help.

"Where are your clubs? We can go play a few holes of golf." She stood.

"I didn't bring any clubs."

"How about tennis? I have racquets."

"No."

"Football?"

"Rosamund, what do you want?" he shouted, using her full name.

"I want you dressed and out of this house," she shouted back. As far as she could remember, they had never been angry with one another.

"Why? Does my being undressed cause a problem for you?"

Yes! She almost shouted the word out loud, but managed to hold her tongue and answer him with a blistering stare.

"If this is your bedside manner, it sucks," he told her.

"You're not in bed." Rose waited a moment, dispelling the image that jumped into her mind at her own words. She spoke in a low voice. "Evan, I can tell something traumatic has happened to you and you're burying it in depression and inactivity. You need to get out, mingle with people, return to the living."

"I don't want to."

She knew that, totally understood from her own experience that he just wanted to crawl in a hole and pull it in after him. But that wouldn't help.

"Isn't that the reason you came here?" He didn't answer her and she didn't expect he would. "Well you're going to have to leave Lighthouse, because I'm not going to let you die in here." The two glared at each other like hungry lions.

"And how do you plan to do that?"

"I got you a job."

"You did what?" His eyes widened in surprise. "I already have a job."

"Not here, and the school needs you."

"What school?"

"Here." She thrust the papers on the counter toward him.

"What are these?"

"They're application papers to be a substitute teacher at the high school."

"You're kidding?" She thought she saw his hands shake more. There was an automatic reaching for a pocket that wasn't there. She wondered what he had in that pocket that he used as an anchor.

"I am not kidding. One of the history teachers had a family emergency. He had to leave Lighthouse to handle it. The school always needs substitutes. You're going to be here a short time. This is a perfect job."

"I don't need or *want* a job."

"You need to be involved with other people. And who better than teenagers? *Their* world is the only one that is important to them. They won't notice yours. You can hide in plain sight."

"You're awful bossy for someone who knows nothing about my situation."

She smiled at him. "Thank you."

"That wasn't a compliment."

"I know it wasn't," she said seriously. "Evan, I know there's something troubling you. Whatever it is, you're not going to fix it by hiding in here."

She spread her arms encompassing the kitchen. "The kids don't know anything about you and they won't probe into what brought you here, like your old friends will." She paused, hoping he would say something but he only took another drink of his juice. "Will you consider it?"

He hesitated a long moment. "Do I have a choice?"

"Of course you do," she said, all the while shaking her head no.

Chapter 2

Evan flexed his hands several times. Nervousness had his palms sweating so badly, the toy rattle nearly slipped through his fingers. Dropping it in his pocket, Evan wiped his brow with a paper towel and washed his hands in the teachers lounge. He could kill Rose for subjecting him to this. In three minutes he had to stand in front of a history classroom and teach. American History from the Pilgrims to World War I. It hadn't changed since he was a student in this same school. He could talk to senators and congressmen without the slightest twitch. But thoughts of facing a room of pimple-faced fifteen-year-olds had him sweating.

Holding his hands out in front of him, he looked for the tremor. It was there, but not so apparent as it had been. *Only their world is important to them.* Rose's words came back to him. He'd come back here to rest and heal. But he had been bored rambling around the big house alone. Intuitively, Rose must have known that. And like the old Rose, she'd taken action. He could have refused. Both of them knew that, but he needed something to occupy his mind. Substituting seemed like an all right idea. He'd once thought of teaching, but that had involved teaching law courses—not high school. And who would think that only a week after turning in the application papers, he'd be called? The wheels in Maine were obviously better oiled than those on Capitol Hill.

Checking his appearance in the mirror mounted on the lounge door, he picked up his books and papers and headed for the classroom. It was sink-or-swim time, he told himself. Rose thought he could do this, but if he fell on his face he'd make sure she was there to cushion him.

"Good morning." He entered the room and placed his papers on the desk. There was an audible gasp when the students saw him.

A young man walking into the room behind

him did a double take and stopped in midstride. "Are you a substitute?" he asked, positioning his body as if Evan's answer would give him reason to turn around and leave.

"Please have a seat," Evan said. The staring contest lasted for two seconds before the young man in oversize jeans and a huge T-shirt took long strides and looped his leg across a desk chair to settle into the saddle.

Take control right away, Rose had told him. The school's seminar for new teachers that he'd attended gave him a few pointers and he intended to try them immediately. He took the chalk and wrote MR. HARPER on the blackboard. "I'll be your teacher today." Then he looked at each face individually, conveying a silent message that there would be no free-for-all in his room.

After he'd subdued the room, Evan opened the history text. "According to the plan left by your teacher, we should be discussing the French and Indian War."

"Do we really have to do that?" A girl, dressed in black from head to toe, asked.

"No, we don't. I'm not required to teach. This is just a glorified babysitting job and you all—" he gestured at the room "—are the babies. I can have you read the text for the next forty minutes while I use the computer to check my stock holdings or e-mail." He glanced at the laptop on the desk. "Or…we can talk about the French and Indian War."

"Aw hell, let's go to war," Big Jeans and Big T-shirt said. The room erupted in laughter.

"Open your text to chapter three." He waited while the general noise level crescendoed and abated. "Are there any questions before we start?"

A hand went up in the back. Evan acknowledged a young man wearing a black sweatshirt with a faded skull on the front.

"What's it like to do what you do?" he asked.

So his identity was known, Evan thought.

"What does he do?" someone else wanted to know.

"He writes speeches for people who can't write," the boy in the back said, only it was punctuated with a silent "stupid" tacked to the end. This came from a blond girl with bright red lipstick.

"Why you wanna know that?" another student asked.

"What?" The boy pumped his chest out and slapped it with both hands like some television hood. "I might wanna be one, one day."

"Yeah, right." Red Lipstick rolled her eyes and a smattering of laughter scattered through the room. It was stemmed by a glare from Faded Skull.

"I can answer that," Evan injected. The room turned to face him as if he was about to impart some great secret. He set his book down and leaned against the front of the desk, crossing his legs at the ankles. "I work for a senator."

"You mean one of those guys in Washington, like the president?"

"Not exactly. I don't write speeches for the president. He has his own staff of writers. And my senator is a woman."

"Get out!" A smiling girl in the front row pumped her fist in the air. A few heads nodded.

"Being a speechwriter is an intense, high-pressure job. The hours are nonstop."

"Why do you do it?" Girl in Black asked, her face crunched in a frown.

"Because it changes lives. I get a sense of satisfaction out of knowing that I'm working for something that benefits us all."

"But my dad says your senator is from Illinois. This is Maine." Laughter broke out loud enough to disturb the next classroom.

From then on the class went well. They didn't exactly follow the lesson plan, but he didn't think that would matter much. For the rest of the day, students came to class asking questions and appeared interested in what Evan had to say. He talked all day, answering questions, explaining a

typical day in his life, reciting some of his
speeches, forgetting his nervousness, forgetting
his early-morning fear of standing before a classroom, and the nightmares that plagued him, but remembering his thoughts of Rose. This time the
thought brought a different kind of fear, but one
which he wouldn't mind exploring.

By the time Evan completed the paperwork for
the returning teacher and signed out in the office, all
the school buses had left the campus and the football
team was practicing in the field behind the school.

Emerging through the front door, Evan was surprised to find Rose sitting on the hood of her Jeep
waiting. She could have passed for a high-school
student waiting for her detention-held boyfriend.
Her face lit up when she saw him coming and a
splinter of joy lightened his heart. Her mink-brown
eyes caught the sun as she waved at him. Rose
hadn't changed much from the young girl she used
to be. Her light brown hair still had a glow to it.
She usually wore it loose around her neck, but
today she'd pulled it off her face, displaying her
square jaw and high cheekbones.

As Evan got closer, he appreciated her whiskey-
colored skin tone and the outdoor look that she
wore with ease.

"Don't you ever work?" he asked, slipping into
the familiar banter they had shared since childhood.

"I'm the doctor. I make my own hours."

"Do you mean people only get sick when you're available?"

"No, I keep them healthy so they don't have to disturb me." She slipped her long, thin body off the polished surface. "How was your first day?"

Evan set his briefcase on the ground next to him. "It went well." He smiled. "I never thought I'd like it."

"But you did?" She clasped her hands together, anticipating his agreement.

Evan nodded. "It was fun."

"I knew it. Come on, I want to hear all about it."

"Wait a minute." He stopped her as she started for the driver's side of the Jeep.

"I have a car in the parking lot." He glanced toward the black SUV sitting among pickup trucks, Jeeps and other SUVs in the faculty parking lot:

"It'll be there. I'll bring you back."

He pushed his briefcase over the seat and let it drop on the floor. "You know, I don't remember you being this bossy before."

"Life happens. People change." She ran around the front end and got in.

"Where are we going?"

"The old lighthouse."

Everyone called it the "old" lighthouse as if there was a newer one that had been built to replace the old one—the only one.

Standing on the rocky Maine coast since 1830, the town took its name from the safety symbol. It stood straight, painted white in the gleaming afternoon sun. The lamp in the zenith of the structure was fully electric and no longer required day-to-day maintenance. No lighthouse keeper was employed by the town. The Coast Guard owned it, but it was managed by a local real-estate office. The two-story house dwarfed by the conjoined lighthouse was rented out during the summer months to tourists who thought it was cool to spend hundreds of dollars for a night in an historic artifact.

Rose pulled the Jeep up near the structure, bypassing the public parking lot. As a local, she had privileges not available to the summer birds. The wind was strong off the Atlantic as they stepped out into the air. Putting her hand up to hold her hair out of her face, Rose was exhilarated by the force of the wind.

"Here," she shouted above the sound of the surf, and threw him a parka and blanket. Evan was wearing a shirt with a pullover sweater and slacks. She knew it would be cold, especially for someone who'd been in D.C. for years and probably spent his days indoors. Although, from what she'd seen of his body, he obviously spent some time in a gym.

Shrugging into the coat, Evan pulled the collar up while Rose covered her head with her hood and tied the drawstring.

"Wow, I forgot how beautiful this could be," Evan said. He stared out to sea, his eyes scanning the gray rock of the Maine coastline. Then he looked up at the lighthouse.

"Ever been up there?" Rose asked.

He nodded. "The Boy Scouts used to paint it every few years. At least up to the point where a ladder would go. The top was always done by a crew from Wanger Painting and Wallpaper. I worked on it twice and, of course, we had to go exploring." He leaned back, taking in the full thirty-three-foot column.

"Of course." She was just as adventurous as he'd been in her youth.

"What about you?"

"Fifth-grade class trip." She smiled at him and pulled her own blanket around her shoulders. Together they sat on the hard stone. When Rose left home to pick up Evan at the high school, the car blanket she kept in her trunk was the only one she had. Realizing closeness might not be something he could handle, she'd retraced her route and got a second blanket. "Speaking of fifth grade, you were going to tell me how school was today."

"Is it time for my report?"

"Just an interested friend." She feigned innocence.

He gave her a sidelong glance and held it for a moment. "It was better than I thought it would be." He quickly told her about the classes, how much he enjoyed being behind the teacher's desk instead of in front of it.

"I was a little surprised at the kids," Evan commented.

"Why?"

"I don't think there was a single person dressed like a student. What happened to sweaters and jeans? I had girls totally in black, boys in clothes several sizes too large, T-shirts or sweatshirts with logos saving everything from Can't Touch That to Have a Nice Day—Sucka. Even the ones I could determine were very intelligent dressed like—" He groped for the right word.

"Evan, you have got to get out of the Capitol Building and look at some MTV."

"We were never like that. If I tried going to school in clothes like that my parents would have barred the door."

Rose laughed. "We had our own way of expressing ourselves. This is theirs. Remember the big hair, gold chains of all sizes and patches sayings things like I'm Old Enough that we used to sew in the most suggestive places?"

Evan smiled and Rose noticed the small crinkles around his eyes. In the daylight she could truly see his handsome features and her heart beat faster.

"I suppose it's the same. They just seem more…out there."

"Don't worry. In time they will become the citizens of tomorrow." She stood when she delivered that phrase, then sat down again.

"Is that who we are now?"

She nodded. He'd suddenly gotten serious. At their graduation ceremony the principal had delivered the corny phrase in a standard graduation speech. At the time they had laughed at it, never thinking they would be the people shaping the world.

After a long moment of silence Evan suddenly laughed.

"What's so funny?" Rose asked.

He related a story about one of the students getting into a verbal discussion about whether people should have to write compositions.

"I gather she didn't like to write."

"Not at all," Evan agreed, his eyebrows going up.

"Did you try to persuade her differently?"

He nodded.

"And did you convince her?"

"I'm not sure." He frowned. "Kids are strange. I can usually tell when I'm getting through to an adult. I can see the exact moment when they begin to believe what I'm saying. It's in their eyes, in the body language. It's like I know."

"But…" She waited for him to go on.

"But they, not only the girl but all of them, they have a language of their own."

"And you're going to learn it?"

His eyes were on Rose. "Yes."

"I *knew* you'd like it," she repeated. "The school is glad to get you."

"Don't be so energetic. It's only the first day."

"It's a start," she said.

The both looked at the water. And they both understood the double meaning of her words.

The scream woke him. Evan sat straight up in bed as if a spring had propelled him forward. His heart pounded and sweat poured over his face and chest. His breath came in hard gasps. "It was the dream," he said to calm himself. "Only a dream."

Relief eased his tight muscles and he flopped back on sweat-damp pillows. The sheet was wrapped around his legs and he fought it to get free. He hadn't recognized the voice, that terrified, horribly helpless sound in his dream, but he knew it was his. He could still feel the hands holding him back, preventing him from entering the blazing building.

Pushing the sheet aside, he rolled to a sitting position. The baby rattle sat on the nightstand. He grabbed it and clung to it, then hung his head in his hands. It was three o'clock in the morning. He thought—hoped—the dream wouldn't come to him here. He'd slept soundly for most of the two weeks he'd been in Lighthouse, gotten involved with the community and actually liked working at the high school. But his mind wasn't ready to let him rest yet. He was haunted by the fire, haunted by his own guilt.

It was his fault.

Gabe had been with Alana, Evan's ex-wife. Evan was an hour late picking him up. Gabe would be alive if he'd been there. No, he stopped himself remembering what the therapist had told him. It wasn't his fault. He couldn't have known what would happen. How many times had he heard that? Why then wouldn't it sink into his brain? Why couldn't he stop thinking that if he'd left the office earlier, if the senator hadn't decided to accept the keynote address at the last moment, if life had been different, his world would be different?

Through the open window the night air cooled the room, drying the sweat on Evan's skin. Getting up, he pulled it down to within an inch of the ledge. The lighthouse stood in the distance, its light searching the seas. Barefoot, Evan padded to the kitchen, flexing his muscles with the stretch of his arms overhead, desperately wanting a distraction to chase away any remnants of the nightmare.

He finished the orange juice, drinking it straight from the container. This time when he pitched the empty carton, it swished into the trash can, touching nothing but air.

It wasn't likely that he'd fall asleep anytime soon. This was the routine he'd lived with since the death of Gabe and his ex-wife, Alana. He'd wake from the dream and remain that way for most of the night. When it was nearly time for him to get up, he'd drift off to sleep. He kept his nightmares and insomnia a secret from anyone at work, brushing it off to overwork whenever someone mentioned that he looked tired. He could handle it, he told himself. The dreams didn't come every night. Most nights he was fine. They got less and less frequent and he was sure he had dealt with the grief.

Then it happened again.

His head ached suddenly, as if he'd been hit by a lightning bolt. He heard the sirens. They were loud, the way they appeared in the dream, but he was awake. They were loud inside his head. He couldn't stop the sound.

Evan closed the refrigerator door and walked through the house. He didn't bother with lights since the lighthouse flooded the sky with its light, brightening the small town. Since it was built, the families in Lighthouse were so used to the intermittent light that it was second nature, almost unnoticeable.

The wind battered the eastward side of the house and Evan heard the surf crashing against the rocks in the distance. For a moment he looked into the darkness, then switched on a light and spied the schoolbooks he'd left on the desk in the den. He was using the room as a combination office and dining room. The formal dining room off the kitchen on the opposite side of the house could seat up to thirty. On holidays or for family gatherings when his aunts, uncles and cousins would come up, the room was bright and gay with decorations and laughter.

Rarely did Evan eat in the den. Rarely was he eating at all. He spied a partially eaten sandwich on a plate he'd set on a small chair. His computer was set up, but he resisted turning it on and checking mail. By now he probably had a thousand messages. When he was in the District, the machine was like an extension of his arm, but here life didn't seem so urgent. And the therapist suggested he put some distance between himself and work. Someone else would have to do it. He picked up the history book. Maybe he could bone up on the significant events of the eighteenth century. He was only a couple of chapters ahead of the class and there was at least one girl in his third period who'd already read farther than he had.

Taking the three-pound book into the living room and sitting in an oversize chair next to a lamp, Evan prepared to read, but something out of the corner of his eye arrested his attention. It was a clear night and the intermittent flashes from the lighthouse glinted off the mailbox at the end of his walkway. Moving to the front door, he looked through the window. The flag on the rural-style box was up, indicating there was mail inside to be picked up. But Evan hadn't left anything in his mailbox.

It only took a second for him to come up with Rose Albright's name. He headed for the door, but his body stopped in midstep as an image of Rose slipped into his mind. His entire being was infused with heat and the beginnings of sexual desire. It surprised him with its intensity. Opening the door, he found the coolness of the air didn't even register on his shirtless frame.

Regaining control of himself, he went to the mailbox. Inside was a single envelope, unsealed and completely blank. He pulled out a card which read, *Pick you up at 9:00 Saturday night. Dress casually. Wear your dancing shoes.* It was signed with a small drawing of a rose.

Evan recognized the way Rose signed her name for friends. She'd been doing it since grade school. It was usually a pen-and-ink drawing, but this one had the petals colored in red and the leaves in green. He looked from the card in his hand to the house next door. Rose's room had faced his when they were in high school. They were close enough to see each other, but too far away to hold a conversation without shouting. The light was off in that room. He didn't know if she still occupied it or if she had moved into larger quarters after her parents retired to the perpetually warm climate of Delray Beach, Florida.

He did know that the girl next door was making his stay here a little more complicated than he'd planned.

Evan started retracing his steps, when a voice stopped him.

"Can't sleep?"

He searched the area for where the voice had come from. Rose stepped from the shadows of her fence railing.

"It's three o'clock in the morning. I could ask you the same thing."

"I asked you first." There was no humor in her statement. He knew she was serious. He knew he was speaking to the doctor, not the friend he'd grown up with.

"It's the quiet. I'm used to more noise on the street." He tried to cover himself with a lie. The darkness helped. She wouldn't be able to see his features clearly.

"How long have you been having trouble sleeping?" She opened the side gate that led to the driveway separating the two properties and came toward him.

"Rose, I'm not your patient. And it's much too cold to discuss this out here." Evan felt the stones under his bare feet and the wind against his naked skin. Although the temperature of his skin increased with each step that brought her closer to him.

"We can go inside." She was standing in front of him now. Only the mailbox separated them. That's if Evan didn't count the invisible barrier he'd erected. Without waiting for him to answer, Rose turned toward the steps.

"Can't this wait until tomorrow?"

"Why? You'll be up for hours."

"How would you know that?" Evan frowned. He'd been hiding his insomnia and his inability to admit something was wrong for so long that he couldn't get used to telling people about it. Even talking to the therapist had taken some time for him to open up completely.

"I've seen the lights on late at night," Rose explained.

"You've been spying on me?"

"Don't be melodramatic, Evan. This is Lighthouse, not D.C. We don't have spies here. Just concerned neighbors."

For a moment he thought they were going to have a standoff in the yard, but she turned and walked toward his open door, leaving him no choice but to follow her.

Inside, he no longer needed a shirt to ward off the cold. Being near her had unleashed the heat of a wood-burning stove in his body. But he needed a minute to collect himself and pulled on a pair of jeans and topped them with a T-shirt that had FBI printed in huge black letters on the front.

Rose was in the kitchen when he returned to the first floor.

"Coffee is the last thing I need," he said.

She turned around with two cups in her hands. "I figured you wouldn't drink warm milk straight, so I made hot chocolate." She headed into his living room and sat on the sofa, placing the cups side by side on the coffee table.

Evan picked up the book he'd left on the chair and laid it on the floor, taking the seat opposite

Rose. He'd spent time while dressing getting himself back in control. He didn't want to waste that effort by sinking down next to her. Taking a cup teeming with marshmallows, he raised his bare feet to the end of the table and sipped. The drink was sweet and hot and sticky, exactly the way he liked it.

"All right, Doc, shoot."

"I'm going to ignore your attitude." She paused. "Why can't you sleep?"

"I don't know."

"I don't believe you."

"Too bad."

Rose leaned forward and set her cup on the table. "Evan, I could look you up on the Internet and probably find something about why you're here. Even though you're standing on the sidelines in Washington, you're still a public figure. There's probably a lot of articles out there with your name in them. It would take a while, but I'm good at reading between the lines."

"So why haven't you?"

Evan stiffened. He knew the article about the fire had been in the back pages of the papers. Him working for a U.S. senator had made it more newsworthy than if he'd been a simple lawyer with an ex-wife and a child. If Rose looked there she'd find that story, but not the one about him in his office.

"I'd like you to trust me enough to tell me. I'm still your friend, even if a few years have gone by."

Guilt laced through him like a white-hot branding iron. Once they had been close enough to cry on each other's shoulders, tell each other their deepest secrets. Evan wasn't sure he was ready to share this one. He wasn't sure he could explain it with the detachment he wanted to achieve. So he swallowed the thought of opening up to her.

"Would you mind if we dropped this conversation?"

"All right," she said, but Evan could see her disappointment in the way her body sank back against the sofa. "Would you like me to write you a prescription for a sleep aid?"

He shook his head. "I don't want any medication."

She nodded and he instinctively knew that she'd determined that he'd already gone that route. And taken it to the brink of addiction.

"Would you like me to recommend someone for you to talk to?"

"I don't need a psychiatrist, psychologist or psychotherapist. I'll handle this in my own way."

"Been there, done that?" she suggested. Her eyebrows raising in inquiry.

He hesitated. He'd already said more than he wanted to say. In fact, he had seen a psychotherapist. After trashing his office, the senator had insisted.

Rose slid off the sofa and came to sit on the table in front of him. Evan put his feet on the floor, sitting forward in his chair to accommodate her. She took his cup and set it behind her. Turning back, she reached for his hands. He had to lean forward, but he dropped his head so as not to look into her eyes. Or let her look into his. He didn't want her to touch him, but pulling his hands away would make it more obvious that they were trembling. As much as he willed them to remain still, they disobeyed like an unruly child.

"Evan, there's no shame in seeking help." Rose's voice was soft. And her mouth was close to him. He could feel her breath on his hair.

"I have what I need. Believe me, I'm working through it." He looked at her then. "Stop playing doctor."

She stared into his eyes. Her hands still held his and they still shook. The rest of his body he held rigidly in check.

"I'll stop playing doctor," she said, raising a hand and running it along the contours of his jaw. "But I'm still your friend."

With that she stood. Evan moved back and she passed him to go to the door. He got up, moving right through her lingering scent. It wasn't perfume, but a clean taste of freshness that he associated with Rose. His body reacted the same way it had when he'd opened the door to the mailbox, and when her voice had come out of the darkness and fissured through him.

After she'd taken his hands in hers, his senses had registered higher on the sensory scale. He could feel her fingers on his in a more elemental way than when two people held hands.

This was unreal, he thought. This was *Rose*. She reached the door.

"Think you can get some sleep now?" she asked.

He was suddenly tired. "I think so."

"Good night then."

"Good night, Rose."

Neither of them moved. For a charged moment they stared at each other.

"See you at nine tonight," she said.

For a moment he was confused, still lost in his thoughts. Then he remembered. "I'll wear my dancing shoes."

Evan had the feeling he was seeing her for the first time, yet knew he'd known her all of his life. He felt himself leaning forward. He wanted to hold her, like he'd done on the bridge. This time he knew who she was. This was Rose.

Chapter 3

At exactly nine o'clock Rose rang Evan's door-bell. She was unsure how to greet him. He was her friend, but she was a doctor and she couldn't see someone in pain and not want to help relieve it. But it was the friendship that caused the dilemma. Where could she draw the line? And why did she need to figure that out? Most of the people in town were her patients. Some she had known as long as she'd known Evan. But her insides didn't ache and her knees didn't turn to water when they walked in a room. And none of them made her mouth go dry at the sight of their bare chests.

When she'd left Evan in the early hours of the morning, he looked tired, drained, and had leaned toward her as if he was going to kiss her. Then he'd stopped. She'd lain awake wondering about that. Did she want him to kiss her? What would she have done if he hadn't stopped?

She thought of Brett and felt a little guilty. Evan wasn't like Brett. Brett had been open, easy to communicate with. He'd defined what-you-see-is-what-you-get. At least he had after he told her about his heart condition. She'd known Evan all her life, had lived next door to him for fifteen years before he left for law school. After that he'd begun his career and rarely came back to Lighthouse. Since then there was a wall between them. She wondered if he'd learned to keep himself aloof, separated from those around him, because of his job in Washington. Or was there some trauma that gave him nightmares and caused the nervousness that had his hands shaking and kept him awake through the night?

Evan opened the door immediately. Rose was startled for a moment. She hadn't expected him to be so quick or to find him standing there looking as good as chocolate. He wore a startlingly white shirt with khaki pants that had creases sharp enough to draw blood. On his feet were the boots he'd worn on the Allison Avenue bridge.

"Do you know this is the first time I've been to your house when you weren't in pajamas?" She regretted the statement as soon as she said it, but he'd jarred her senses standing there framed in the door. Backlit by the foyer's chandelier, the white shirt contrasted with his dark, scented skin. He was clean shaven and looked as if he'd had a haircut. *Sexy* and *gorgeous* were the words that came to mind.

Evan's expression changed at her comment. She felt more than saw the tension in him. "Which do you prefer?" he asked, his voice laced with sexual innuendo.

"Maybe we'd better go." She didn't wait for a reply, but turned and headed past the empty rocking chairs to the Jeep in her driveway. She could feel Evan staring at her. She knew he was laughing, but she didn't join in the joke. The thought of him in those drawstring pajamas caused a rush of emotion she was unwilling to confront.

"I take it we're going to a party?" he said when they were seated in the car and she headed toward the center of town.

"You go to parties in D.C. Up here it's a dance."

"Where is this dance?"

"Kings Ballroom."

"That place is still open?"

"You won't recognize it. They've completely

renovated the building. I think the Kings did it to attract all the new arrivals in the area."

"I noticed the town has expanded. There are even some places the light doesn't reach. I thought there was a law saying if the light didn't touch your house, you weren't in Lighthouse."

Rose laughed as she drove. "With the expansion of the food-processing plant more residents moved to the area. They had to have housing and entertainment."

Kings Ballroom had been a small restaurant with neon signs and a downstairs room for dancing when Evan lived in Lighthouse. The building that Rose pulled up in front of had a semicircle entrance with a dark green canopy announcing its name in white letters, valet parking and no neon. She got out, handing her keys to the parking lot attendant.

"Hi, Dr. Albright."

"Hi, Billy."

"Hey, you must be Mr. Harper, the speechwriter." He was poised to take the seat Rose vacated.

"Guilty," Evan replied.

"Nice to meet you." Billy abandoned his position and walked around the Jeep to shake Evan's hand. "We've heard a lot about you since you got back."

Rose joined the two men and explained. "This

is Billy Campbell. Margie Campbell's younger brother."

Margie had graduated high school with Rose. Billy was only a year old at the time, but everyone in the Campbell family had the same look, thick red mops of hair and ruddy complexions. It was as if they had all been tapped out of matching molds, some with longer hair than others.

"You were only a baby."

"I'm in high school now, only not in any of your classes," Billy said. "I kinda wish I were."

"Why is that?" Rose asked.

"Boy, you should hear the guys talk about the stuff he teaches." He indicated Evan. "It's nothing like my dry old history teacher." Billy screwed his freckled, acne-covered face into a frown. "You must have lived the history. Oh, I don't mean you're that old…I mean…"

"It's alright, Billy. I understand what you mean," Evan said.

"Well, I just wish I were."

"Good night, Billy," Rose said, ending the conversation.

"Oh, good night, doctor. Nice seeing you, Mr. Harper." He started for the driver's side of the car.

Evan put his hand on the small of Rose's back and guided her toward the door. She felt the warmth go right through her.

"You said they renovated. They must have razed this place and built it from the ground up."

"They did," she replied.

The room that held the Saturday-night crowd had a large square bar in the center with stools all the way around it. Glassware hung from racks overhead. There was a local band playing on a raised bandstand and couples gyrating on the dance floor.

"This is different," Evan stated. "They have a real dance floor."

Rose laughed. She felt as if the tension that had been coiled inside her since Evan opened his door relax a bit. The room was no longer downstairs. It looked out on a grassy lawn with fountains and gazebos where wedding photos were often taken. The windows were huge on one side of the room. It had no resemblance to the previous bar and bare floor space they used to dance on before the Kings rebuilt the place.

"Let's see if we can find a table," Evan suggested.

"We already have a table." A voice from behind them spoke. They turned and found the smiling face of Matthew Haynes.

"Matt, what are you doing here?" Evan asked as the two men clasped hands and embraced. Then Matt kissed Rose on the cheek.

"I was in the neighborhood." Matt was a

systems engineer at MIT. "The truth is, I talked to my mom and she told me you were back. Claudia and I jumped in the car and here we are."

Matt turned and they headed for the table he was holding. Matt and Evan had been in the same classes in high school and both went off to college together, but Evan went to law school while Matt married his high-school sweetheart and made his mark as a computer geek. He looked more like a football player than someone who spent his days in front of a machine designing the next generation of computer processors.

Brett came to Rose's mind for the second time that night. She put her hand on her stomach as a wave of grief passed through her. While Matt was healthy and athletic looking, Brett had been pale and thin. Matt, like Evan, never really took to being a sports participant, but unlike Evan, Matt was a spectator at heart, never giving up tickets to any New England team event.

"Claudia!" Evan called as his strides increased. Matt's wife was sitting at the table they were heading toward. She stood and Evan swallowed her in a bear hug.

"Evan, it's good to see you again," she said.

"Thanks for coming up," he said.

"We were coming for the Final Day sail, but when we heard you were here, we had to come see you. It also gives our families the chance to see us twice in a short period of time. And I'm glad Matt's taking a break."

"Well, I'm glad you came." Evan knew his friend was a workaholic. When he got onto a problem that needed solving, it was hard to get his attention for anything else.

"Why don't we sit down," Rose suggested, but before they could take their seats, several mutual friends came up and the round of hellos began again.

"Hey, Doc, you wanna dance?" Jerry Longfellow, one of the town deputies asked. She looked at Evan, but he was ensconced in a conversation with his old friends and didn't see her.

"Sure, Jerry. I'd love to."

Once she was on the floor, she stayed there. Since she knew virtually everyone in town, it appeared they all wanted to dance with her. One dance led to another and another. Each time she looked at Evan he was talking to someone and paying no attention to her. His ignoring her shouldn't have affected her, made her angry, but it did.

Finally she left the floor and headed for the table. No one was sitting since the crowd had grown well beyond the number of chairs available. Evan reached for her hand almost without looking at her. He put a drink in it, but not before she felt the tremor in him. She was breathing hard and very thirsty. He seemed to know it and she forgave him for ignoring her, realizing that he knew where she was all the time. The knowledge made her heart sing. Lifting the drink to her mouth, she tasted ginger ale and downed it in great gulps.

Then she looked at him. He was sweating and he dabbed at his face with a handkerchief. She'd been dancing and she was hot, but she knew his heat came from another source. She had to get him out of there.

"Excuse me, Spike." She interrupted another of their friends who was talking about an old football charge during a long-forgotten game. "I need to talk to Evan a moment."

"Sure, Rose."

She took Evan's arm and led him toward a back exit that put them out on a patio in front of the expanse of lawn.

She heard Evan sigh as they stepped into clear air. He walked a few steps away from her and took a deep breath. "What do you want to talk to me about?"

"Nothing."

"Nothing? Then why did—" He stopped, realizing her ploy. "You rescued me?"

"You looked like you needed it." They walked to a gazebo and went up the steps. Rose ran her fingers along the painted wood surface and thought of the brides and grooms who'd used this building to capture photos of the best day of their lives. There was no moon tonight. From the gazebo no one could see them. Rose walked around the circle and stopped near the steps. Evan sat on the banister, holding one of the support poles.

"They ask a lot of questions," he finally said.

"They don't mean anything by it. They're—"

"I know. It's being friendly, catching up on the time since we last saw each other. I didn't want to lie, but I also didn't want to go into detail."

She understood. He still hadn't told her what had brought him back to Lighthouse, and Rose knew it had to be serious. She wanted to know but stopped herself from prying. When he wanted her to know, he would tell her.

"We'll just stay out here a while and then we can go back in or leave."

"This is fun for you. I saw you dancing." He'd channeled the conversation to her, away from himself. Rose gave in to his evasion.

"I like to dance. I always did." She felt defensive. "And you didn't ask me."

"I didn't get the chance."

"Well?"

"Would you like to dance?" he asked.

"I would love to."

He moved toward her. Rose was suddenly apprehensive. She'd been in his arms once, on the bridge. The feelings that went through her when she thought about him were unusual. Actually being held by him, out here in the dark, under a moonless sky, could undo her usual detachment.

"We're not going to dance out here?" She looked over her shoulder at the windows and dancers inside.

"I thought we'd try the dance floor."

She was relieved only slightly. Out here they'd be alone, and that could have her communicating more of her feelings than she wanted. Inside there were more people, but she didn't know if she'd be safer once his arms closed around her.

"Let me see your hands," she said.

"What?"

She opened hers, palms up. "Give them to me." Evan placed his hands in hers. The tremor could barely be felt. He knew she was checking his stress quotient. "Are you sure? I mean, don't play the macho man with me. I'm a doctor."

"Come on, Doctor, you can diagnose me on the dance floor." He slipped an arm around her waist and pulled her along with him.

Opening the door brought them back to loud music and laughter. The deep bass rhythm had people moving fast and wild. The song ended as Evan turned Rose into his arms. The sudden cessation of music had couples collapsing into each other, clapping and wiping sweat from their faces and arms. Some left the floor in search of drinks.

The band moved smoothly into a ballad. Rose didn't make the transition quite as fast. She stopped as the first strains of "A House is Not a Home" began to play. She'd heard the band play that song before and their rendition of it, which she'd always enjoyed, was at least ten minutes long. Ten minutes in Evan's arms. She'd slow danced with him before, but that was a lifetime ago. They were no longer the same people. The song brought it home to her. They'd both been married and suffered traumas. Maybe they were lonely and gravitating toward each other. Maybe it was chemistry alone, but there was something that frightened her, and for the next ten minutes she would be tested to keep it to herself.

They were adults, no longer the teenagers whose every little incident was steeped in drama. Yet at this moment, Rose felt the drama. She turned to leave the dance floor, intent on waiting for the next fast-and-free rhythm. But Evan took her hand and turned her back to him. She opened her mouth to speak, but Evan slipped his hand around her waist and pulled her body into sharp contact with his. She gulped, her head snapping up to look at him, her mind incapable of rational thought.

With his touch, Rose felt the room and the crowd recede. Only the music remained. The two of them were alone, not just in the bar but in the world. She knew this with her heart. As his legs moved, she followed him, his steps as easy to match as if she were shadow dancing in her living room.

His arms were strong around her, yet he guided her steps with a lightness so sure she felt as if they were suspended in air. His hand caressed hers. Their bodies aligned and Rose gave herself over to the dance, to being in his arms. She leaned into him, laying her head on his shoulder. Her eyes closed. She hummed lightly, feeling her heart merging with his.

Evan's breath lightly fanned her ear and sent a hot shiver down her spine. His touch sent heat washing through her body. Her nerve endings snapped to electrified attention. She didn't understand what was happening to her and she didn't care. She liked the way she felt.

Euphoric.

Exuberant.

Lighthearted.

Alive.

She wanted to scream to the heavens, show her

smile to the world. She felt she could do anything as long as the dance went on and on.

Evan kept one hand on Rose's back as they danced, then slowly moved it up to the bare nape of her neck, slowly caressing her. Rose's mouth went dry. She opened it to take in air, forcing it into her lungs and breathing in the scent of Evan with it. She had no sense of space or time, only the feel of his arms holding her, his fingers entwined with hers, the lightness of his breath and the music wrapping around them, insulating them from the outside world.

Moving his head back, Evan looked into her eyes. His mouth was only a kiss away. His eyes were dark and passionate and she was lost in them. Their stare went on forever. Then, just as Evan closed the distance between them, the world righted itself. The lights came back, the noise of the crowd returned, the band ended the song. She was no longer dancing among the stars, but stood grounded in reality. Conscious of their gang watching them, her arms slid down from Evan's shoulders and she reluctantly stepped out of his arms.

For a moment they stared at each other, still connected. Then someone jostled them and without a word, but by mutual agreement, they returned to the table. Rose knew he'd been affected by the dance, by something intangible between them. She also knew neither of them would discuss it.

"Are you sailing on Final Day, Evan, or just spectating?" Matt asked as Evan held a chair for Rose.

"I hadn't thought about it," Evan said.

"Remember that Final Day back in high school?" Clarence Brown, a friend from their high school days, asked. "When May Goodwin and Kenny Porter sailed the boat they'd built over three summers?" Everyone laughed, remembering what happened to them. "They weren't out ten minutes before the thing blew over and dumped them into the cold water."

"I think I'll watch the regatta from the lighthouse," Evan said, taking a drink of his ginger ale.

"What about you, Rose? Don't you want to sail? You and Evan did a great job back in—"

"Matt, that was a hundred years ago," Rose interrupted. "Besides, I have to be in the medical unit in case there's an accident."

"I forgot. It's hard thinking of you as the town doctor," Matt said.

"Why?" Evan asked. "It's what's she's wanted since we were in school."

"I thought you wanted to be a surgeon in a big hospital," Claudia stated with raised eyebrows.

"I did, but things change. I'm needed here, in Lighthouse. Doc Kidd is retiring. And the town needs a doctor." She shrugged. "I'm it."

"So you've given up the dream?" Claudia asked.

"Not so much given it up as exchanged it for another one." Rose felt exposed. She was hot and not from dancing. She didn't like being in the spotlight and everyone was looking at her. "With Doc gone, what happens to the town if I go back to school for surgery?"

"Rose, you can't carry the weight of the town on your shoulders," Evan said.

"It's not fair to you," Claudia agreed. "What about the clinic and new doctors Doc has been talking about hiring?"

"So far it's just talk. And Doc is leaving, moving to Arizona where he'll be near his daughter and grandchildren."

"I know he's been the only doctor in Lighthouse for years. Maybe it's time to put pressure on the council to move on the issue," Evan suggested.

"Doc tries, but the council has other priorities at the moment." It would be easier to stop the ocean from pounding the rocks below the lighthouse, Rose thought, than to get the council to deal with the real problems facing the citizenry. She'd sat in some of those meetings and they were a waste of time.

Rose would be the lone doctor when Doc left. She didn't often let that thought intercede into her mind or dwell on its impact on her future. But looking at her friends, at Evan, at those who had left the small community to seek their place in the world, she felt as if her wings had been tied down by Doc's hands, the council's hands and by her own.

Evan's feet pounded under him. He jogged over the rocky coastline, moving closer and closer to the lighthouse. He'd jogged practically every day since high school. It was a way of clearing his head and getting things in order for the day. Only it wasn't working. He ran faster, checking the coastline, careful of his feet and the rocks. With every step Rose was still in his mind. What had happened to him last night? Since he'd crossed the Allison Avenue bridge, it was as if he'd stepped into a different world. But he was the same person. Wasn't he?

Not if he judged it by his dance with Rose. They were friends. Nothing more. So why had he held her as though she meant the world to him? Why did he want to run his hands through her hair and pull her mouth to his?

Evan stopped running. He was at the lighthouse. He bent over, his hands on his thighs as his breath came hard and fast. His pulse throbbed and he knew it wasn't all due to his run. After a moment he stretched his legs and started walking in circles. He walked through the parking lot and over to the keeper's house, then back to the tower. By then his heart rate was normal, even if his mind was still racing.

He looked at the rocks where he'd had lunch with Rose. It was too windy and cold for him there after his run. He sat on a visitors' bench and looked at the tower. It needed painting.

What was he going to do? Evan asked himself. He was only going to be here for three months. It was unfair to start a relationship he couldn't finish.

And with Rose.

She deserved better. Last night, while she'd gone to the ladies' room, Claudia and Matt told him what happened to her. She'd only told him her husband died. She didn't tell him the whole truth, but then neither had he opened the compartments to the pain in his own heart.

"She looks so much happier," Claudia had said. "Does that have anything to do with you?"

"What do you mean?" Evan diverted her question.

"Did she tell you about Brett Patterson?" Matt asked.

"Who's Brett Patterson?"

A look passed between husband and wife that said they had a story for him. They told him that while Rose was a resident in Boston, she fell in love with a man named Brett Patterson, a computer engineer who designed software and consulted.

"He was good too, a real genius," Matt went on. "He could see problems in thousands of lines of code that no else would even attempt. MIT tried to get him on their staff, and we weren't the only ones. But he refused."

"Why?"

"He had a heart problem and worked from home," Claudia said.

"Yet he still had a client list that ranked with the Fortune 100," Matt added.

"He sounds too good to be true," Evan said, his voice a little flat. Evan checked the direction in which Rose had gone. He was feeling things that didn't seem right for him. Rose was his friend and he wanted her to be happy.

"When things got serious between them," Claudia picked up the story, "he told her he had a heart problem. They were married in a quiet ceremony with only a couple of people from the hospital and her parents. As a surprise, a few of the nurses planned a reception for the newlyweds. Brett died several months later."

"Brett was a wealthy guy," Matt said. "Apparently he'd changed his will and insurance polices and Rose was the sole beneficiary. She could go anywhere she wanted, but she came here."

Home, Evan thought. He understood her decision to return to Lighthouse. Home is the one place that welcomes you with open arms, where you can go safely and lick your wounds. He was here licking his for three months. Rose had come back permanently.

"Has she been in that house ever since?" he asked.

"Her mom came and stayed with her for a couple of months after she finished her residency in Boston. Since then she's been all doctor."

The pounding surf hit the rocks and water splashed up over the flat surface. The noise brought his attention back to his surroundings. Rose understood his pain more than he realized. She'd said you never forget, but you learn to live with the pain. For Evan it had been two years. For her less than one. She was already living with the pain. He couldn't inflict more on her, he thought. He stood up and did a few more stretching exercises. It would be unfair to continue to let her fall in love with him. He wasn't sure he wasn't falling for her too, but if he was, it was time to stop.

For both their sakes.

Taking a final look at the lighthouse, Evan started to walk down the hill toward his house. It was the last one on the block and the one closest to the lighthouse. Rose's loomed large and white next to his. When he reached his mailbox, he sighed with relief. Rose's car wasn't in her driveway. Turning, he looked back at the light-house and the ocean beyond. He needed to keep out of her way.

And to keep her out of his.

Chapter 4

Final Day arrived on a bright, sunny morning in September. Excitement throughout the hamlet had been going on for a week. It would culminate tonight at the annual town dance. Evan hadn't asked Rose to go with him. It was understood they would go together. She'd been constantly by his side since his arrival, and despite his efforts, it was impossible to avoid her in a town the size of Lighthouse. Their friends had seen them together. Their dance at Kings had been witnessed by people with nothing better to do than make assumptions. For them it seemed natural that he would bring Rose to the dance.

Most of the day she'd be in the mobile medical unit. There was always a scraped knee or arm that needed mending from someone falling on the rocks or jostling in the stands. Few serious accidents happened on the water. It was the spectators whose exuberance called for medical attention.

Rose had already gone when Evan walked the short distance to the lighthouse grounds. Portable stadium seating had been erected and all the seats on it were taken or saved. He waved at Claudia and Matt, wedged together on the top row.

People were camped out on lawn chairs, folded blankets or heavy crates to see the spectacular water show. He saw Spike and his wife with their kids. Jeff Altman, a member of the township committee dressed inappropriately in a suit and tie, worked the crowd as if he were up for reelection.

The air was crisp with a light wind, perfect sailing weather. The boats had been launched and their billowing sails made a beautiful scene against the blue water. Everything from catboats to schooners floated below. Some were distinguishable by the color of their sails. Evan's boat had had a bright red-and-green sail the years he'd participated in the races.

"Evan, over here," Doc Kidd called, making room on the bench next to him. The two men shook hands as Evan seated himself. "Heard you were back. Be here long?"

"A few months."

Doc spoke in short sentences. His cadence was quick and Evan found he'd missed hearing it.

"Dianne and Stephen still in Egypt, I guess?"

"They are. I spoke to them last week." Dianne and Stephen were Evan's parents. His father was the ambassador to Egypt. His parents had been there for the last five years.

"Give 'em my regards. Sorry I'm not going to see them before I leave."

"Rose tells me you're moving to Arizona."

"First of the year if all goes well."

"I thought you'd stick around and build that hospital you've been talking about."

Doc smiled. "I've talked about that a lot over the years. Never quite got time to put anything in the works. Someone else will have to do it now."

"Sorry to hear that. With Lighthouse expanding so rapidly, it could use another doctor."

Doc glanced out at the water. "Rose'll do all right," he said. "Can't think of a better person to leave in charge. She grew up here. Understands the town."

The boats were sailing in formation. Several of them had formed a long line and with the sound of a foghorn they started. It was a race, but the boats moved as if set to music. The crowd got into it, rooting for their favorite. Catboats were always the first race of the day. The high-school kids made the most noise, cheering for one of their own.

Evan and every person in Lighthouse knew the history of Final Day. It had been around longer than anyone living. It honored the end of the fishing season and was a celebration of those who'd ventured into the unknown waters and returned safely, and for those who'd died during their last sojourn. Lighthouse had been a small fishing village in the 1800s, but most of the towns-people now worked at the food-processing plant. Still, the institution existed and it was celebrated, but more with a happy countenance than the surface smiles that were on the faces of those who'd lost family members during the heyday of the whaling era.

"Why aren't you in the medical wagon?" Evan glanced over his shoulder. The white medical unit in the form of a trailer with a huge red cross on its side was parked at the edge of the crowd. Rose was standing near the open door watching the race. Evan couldn't stop himself from looking at her. He gravitated toward her as if some force projected him in her direction. He knew he shouldn't get involved, shouldn't let anything happen more than friendship. But their friendship had never been casual. It was deep and unconditional. Rose waved at him with a smile and he waved back.

"We're taking turns," Doc Kidd said. "Rose is on duty now. I get an hour here. Then I relieve her."

"Seems fair," Evan said. His heart fluttered a moment. He wasn't sure why. Was it Rose's wave or the fact that he could spend some time with her while Doc Kidd took over the medical duties?

Evan couldn't help the feeling that came over him when he thought of spending time with her. In the past, when he'd lived here and she was next door, they'd spent as much time together as any dating couple, but they hadn't been a couple. He'd been entranced with Holly Houseman during high school. And Rose had dated Lance Christian, Tom Adams and Taylor Welling. When had their friendship changed into something more?

And why?

The race ended to cheering crowds. Evan knew from his time as a sailor that the finish line was a white outcropping of rock that could only be seen from the ocean side of the water. There would be several more races, sloops, ketches, yawls and finally the schooners. Then a short closing procession circling the water in a practiced formation before all the boats sailed single file into the marina several miles away.

"Hear you're bringing Rose to the dance," Doc said.

Evan wondered where he'd heard that. "I suppose," he answered noncommittally.

"You two getting pretty close."

Evan wondered where this was going. What did Doc mean? His tone was a little too much like that of a protective father.

"I suppose," Evan replied.

"Be careful," Doc continued. "You're only going to be here for a minute. Don't go starting something you're not prepared to stop."

"Doc, Rose and I are friends. We've been friends since we were in the cradle."

"I know," Doc said. But the message in the two simple words reinforced Doc's warning.

Evan glanced at Rose again. She was looking out at the water, but it looked as if her mind wasn't on the ships or the sails. He wondered what she was thinking about and why it made her look so sad. Since his return, he'd wondered where the old Rose was. Initially he thought she was there, the way she quickly organized him into teaching at the high school, then taking him to Kings, but when she didn't think anyone was looking she'd disappear, crawl inside herself, leaving only a shell.

Knowing he should say something to Doc, Evan looked at the older man but couldn't come up with anything to explain his need to be near Rose.

Evan got up and sauntered over to where Rose

stood, drawn as if by a magnet. He didn't call out to her or indicate that he was coming. He didn't analyze why, only that he didn't want to disturb her thoughts. He wanted to know what she was thinking. She didn't hear him, her concentration was so directed on wherever her mind was. He got close to her, within a step, and she still hadn't turned to acknowledge his presence. He wondered what or *who* she was thinking of. A pain nipped at his heart. Was her state of distraction due to her dead husband? Or had she been thinking of the changes in their relationship?

He knew if he called her name or if he touched her shoulder she would jump. When she came back from wherever she was, he also knew his sudden appearance, as if he'd materialized on the spot, would startle her. There was an option he had that wouldn't scare her. So he opted for her name.

"Rose."

Even though he whispered it, she jumped. Her hand went to her heart as she turned to him. Immediately her smile was in place. "Evan, you scared me."

"Where were you?"

"What?"

He knew she was using the question as a ploy to buy herself time.

"I was here, watching the sails and the sea," she said.

"You were someplace far away."

"Just back in time," she said. "I was remembering the last time I was out on the water for Final Day."

"Good luck or bad luck?"

"It was good. It was just before I left for medical school. My dad was at the controls. We were leading, going fast. I knew we were going to win. Then a sudden gust of wind came up and I couldn't hold the sails. The wind tipped us into the drink."

She smiled, but Evan knew she was lying. The memory she gave him *was* good, but the look on her face hadn't indicated that, even if she was remembering going into the cold water.

"Everyone assumes you're going to the dance with me tonight." Evan didn't know why he said that. He didn't really want to bring up the subject of the dance, but he needed to say something and the words were out before he knew it.

Her gaze was steady, straight into his eyes. Hers caught the sunlight and it brightened them to a clarity that told Evan he could look into her soul if she'd permit it.

"Am I?" she asked in a voice as soft as the breeze.

Doc Kidd's words echoed in his mind, but Rose's clear eyes erased them. Each time Evan saw her he wondered what it was about her that connected with him. Why he wanted to explore every single thought that concerned her. Why his logic seemed senseless when he was near her. And why he said words he never expected to say.

"I'd consider it an honor."

Rose whirled around several times in front of the mirror in her bedroom. She hadn't been to the Final Dance in years. When she lived in Boston, she hadn't come home for it and it was already over when she returned for good last year. People started talking about it, preparing for it right after the July Fourth holiday. As September approached, the town was consumed with talk of the festivities. Rose had ignored it all. While she lived at the base of the lighthouse, her street was accessible by foot only. Until Doc Kidd had told her about the medical unit, she'd planned to spend the day quietly at home and not attend the dance at all.

But then Evan had returned. And she'd danced with him at Kings. She wanted to do that again. She wanted to be held in his arms and charmed around the dance floor. And she wanted to melt into the music.

The doorbell rang and Evan stood waiting as she opened it.

"Wow!" he said when he saw her. "You look beautiful."

Rose was a little embarrassed at the way he was looking at her, but she was pleased she'd decided on the red dress. It was strapless, clung to her body, and had a short chiffon jacket that ended just under her breasts. She'd pulled her hair off her face and coiled it up into a mass of curls, leaving one long section which she'd turned into a curled braid that fell down the side of her face.

"Shall we go?" Rose asked. Evan moved back and she followed him to the SUV where she slipped into her seat and Evan closed the door. It felt close inside the cab, as if a heater had been turned on and she and Evan were inside it. Rose wanted to say something but could think of nothing. She felt like a schoolgirl on her first date.

The dance was in full swing when they got there. Evan helped her out of the SUV and pulled her arm through his. Rose hadn't felt this good in years. She didn't bother to try to free herself. She never wanted to be freed again. Her arm was warm and Evan made her feel as if the two of them were the only people in the room.

He turned her onto the dance floor and whirled her around until she was winded.

"I didn't know you could dance so well," Rose said.

"Neither did I." Evan's voice was happy. "It must be my partner."

Rose hadn't danced this well either. Evan swept her off her feet and swung her around. When he set her straight, she went back into the practiced steps they'd learned years earlier. She knew the dance wouldn't have been so much fun without him there. She followed his movements flawlessly. The music ended abruptly. With a laugh and Evan pulling her into his arms, they hugged as naturally as two lovers.

"Want a drink?" he asked, pushing her back.

Rose nodded and off they went to quench their thirst. "I can't remember when I've danced so hard," Rose said.

"Did you enjoy it?"

"Yes," she said, winded. She took the glass Evan handed her and drank deeply.

She said it as if the memory had just been reinforced, that she didn't remember how much she enjoyed something. But she saw danger in her choices. Evan was home for only a short while, but he was a live wire when she got near him. With only rudimentary coaxing he could burst into flame, taking her with him.

Life in Lighthouse was different from what Evan was used to. He'd walked to town hall right after school on Monday and come out an hour later with all the permits and instructions he needed to begin painting the lighthouse. In D.C. it would have taken an act of Congress to get a simple permit. Evan could begin painting immediately, except Wanger Painting and Wallpaper had to build the scaffolding and Evan needed to complete his design and buy the paint.

As he walked into the paint store, he expected to see Mr. Wanger, but no one he recognized was there.

"I need to give this order to Mr. Wanger," he told the twenty-something.

The young man took the permit and looked at it. "He's in the back. I'll give it to him."

Evan looked around after the man disappeared. The place wasn't totally empty. There were a few people in the aisles. Evan began picking up paint in five-gallon containers. He stacked six of them in front of the counter and went back for brushes, rollers, noseguards and other necessary painting utensils.

"This is for the lighthouse?" The voice spoke from behind him. Evan turned to see the young clerk and Mr. Wanger standing near an open door that led to the stockroom.

"Mr. Wanger." Evan walked toward him, his hand extended.

"Evan Harper." He took his hand in a strong

grip, one that denied his age. He was years older than Evan remembered him and looked shorter. His hair had receded until his crown was smooth and freckled. Hair curved around the back of his head like gray earphones looking for an MP3 player.

"It's an order to build the scaffolding."

"The town's finally going to paint the old girl?" He grinned. "It's been a while and she needs it." He looked down at the order again. "I'll have it up by the end of next week."

"That'll work," Evan said.

"You've got a lot of paint here." Mr. Wanger glanced at him. "Why the red? You aren't thinking of changing the color, are you?"

"It's been white as long as I can remember—"

"As long as I can remember, too," Mr. Wagner interrupted. "And long before that. In fact, that's the only color it's ever been."

"Why is that?"

"I don't know." He looked perplexed. "'Cause that's the color it was originally painted."

"That was back in the 1800s. It's time for a change."

"Folks round here don't take much to change. You know that. You were born and raised here. 'Course, you been down in the government a long time."

Evan heard the veiled threat. "Some of them might like it."

"You go ask them and see what you get." Evan noticed the challenge in Wagner's voice.

"Maybe I will." He kept his voice from showing any disagreement. "Charge the paint to the town account. It's on the work order."

"You sure about this?" Mr. Wanger looked at the paper again. "It don't say nothing here about red paint."

"It says nothing about white either."

Evan didn't want the lighthouse to be plain white in color. The community had lived with it for over a century, mostly because that was the only color paint available in large enough quantities in 1830. Evan planned to change it. The design in his head called for bright yellow and red, along with the traditional white. He wanted ships to be able to distinguish the lighthouse, not just the light.

And after more than a hundred and fifty years, it was time for a change.

Life changes. Hadn't his life been irrevocably altered? Hadn't it for all of them? Mr. Wanger was older. Rose had become a doctor, married and lost a husband. Evan had lost an ex-wife and a child. The town had grown, bringing in people who weren't native to Lighthouse.

They all had to learn to live with change. Even in Lighthouse. Sometimes it could be positive. And that's how he looked at painting the light-house. First, he was doing it alone. And second, it would keep him away from Rose.

It didn't take long for word to spread through town. Evan hadn't had phone service restored to the house, but the lack of a phone number didn't stop the citizenry from stopping him on the street, in the grocery store, on the school grounds or jogging through town to give their opinion on his planned color scheme.

"I hear you're going to paint the lighthouse," Abby Clemson said Tuesday morning as he entered the school office. She was the secretary. Usually busy at her computer when Evan came in to collect the notes in his mailbox, today she seemed to be waiting for him.

He sighed and asked, "Which side are you on? The we've-always-done-it-that-way group or the it's-time-for-a-change section? It's not like I'm running for office. It's only paint."

He didn't wait for an answer. Class discussion was a total bust that day. Everyone coming in wanted to discuss the color of the lighthouse. In between classes he had to debate the virtues of change. There were, however, some people on his side, mainly students who agreed with him because their parents had taken the keep-it-the-same position and they were practicing the rebellious-teenager play.

As he left the building after classes, instead of finding Rose sitting on the hood of her Jeep, he was greeted by a committee from the township.

"This doesn't look good," Evan said as he approached the group of three. He pressed the button on his key to release the lock and automatically slide the side door of the SUV open. He dropped his jacket and briefcase inside and clicked the button for the door to close.

"Evan, we heard what you're planning to do to the lighthouse," Jeff Altman said.

"You guys often conduct business in the parking lot of the high school?" He looked from one to the other, Jeff, Hank Becker and Doris Sorensen.

"This is serious," Doris said. "Do you know how many calls my office has received since this rumor began?"

"No, how many?"

She took a step back, her mouth sputtering, affronted that he would even ask her to quantify her accusation.

"I can tell you it's been a significant number."

"Evan, you can't unilaterally decide to change a tradition that's been around since life began here."

"Come on, Hank, you can't be comparing the beginning of life to a lighthouse."

"All right." Hank frowned and hunched his shoulders. He had a habit of twitching his shoulder when he was nervous. It had nothing to do with any organic ailment. It was clear to Evan that Hank wasn't entirely on sure footing. "I may have been a little over the top, but you understand my meaning."

"No, Hank, I don't. I got the permits and the rules. Nowhere does it say I have to use white paint. Now, if you'll excuse me, I have an appointment."

Evan slipped into the driver's seat and started the engine. He didn't have anyplace to be, but he wasn't going to stand around a parking lot, with a crowd gathering, discussing a subject he'd already been defending for two days.

"This isn't over," Jeff said. "We'll see what the council has to say about it."

Evan stomped on the gas petal, moving too fast. Tires squealed as he turned on to the street and he knew he'd left a layer of rubber on the road behind him. He didn't need this. When he'd thought of painting the lighthouse, he'd never envisioned it causing this much controversy.

Getting the permits might have only taken an hour, but wading through the physical red tape of his friends and neighbors' opinions was altogether different. He was supposed to be resting, playing golf, reading; instead, he was embroiled in a fight over something as insignificant as white paint. Why didn't he just give up? If they wanted it white, he could paint it white. This was his effort, his manpower, his sweat. He wasn't one to back away from an argument. He'd never done that, but he understood a pissing contest and this had all the earmarks of two equally-sized bulls pulling on opposite ends of the same rope.

How long had the tower stood there needing paint, with no one stepping forward to volunteer? The town council hadn't thought to commission anyone to do it either. Now that he'd agreed to the task, everyone had an opinion. And threatening him with a council meeting. Evan sneered at the thought. They had no idea whom they were dealing with. He'd written persuasive speeches before. Just let them try it. He'd run rings around the council. If they wanted a confrontation, he'd give them a show worthy of a New England lawyer. Bring it on, he thought. He was ready.

The traffic light ahead of him turned yellow. Evan hesitated, his foot jumping back and forth between the accelerator and the brake. There was a vehicle coming in the opposite direction with a right signal on. Evan needed to make a left. Quickly he calculated the distance. The fact was, the other car needed to slow almost to a stop to make the turn. He could make it, he thought. Evan pushed the accelerator in. A left turn, two blocks, a right and his house stood at the end of the block. Only a hop from the controversial lighthouse. He didn't want to wait. He didn't want to have to encounter another opinionated resident sitting in a car next to him, someone who'd blow his horn, feeling the need to impart his opinion during the space of time it took for the red light to change to green.

Evan miscalculated. The sound of the horn came too late. He was already into the turn. Suddenly he felt as if he was on a carnival ride, where everything was moving fast, but he could see so much more. There was no time to stop. No time to change his mind. The other car, going right, was headed for the same space.

Evan cursed.

His foot jammed the brake in, pushing it solidly until he was practically standing on it. The back of the SUV fishtailed, spinning around at least thirty degrees. The driver of the other car tried to stop, but momentum and the laws of physics carried it forward as the black hulk of Evan's vehicle hurtled toward it. The SUV came to a stop inches from the grille of the oncoming vehicle.

Evan held his breath. He gripped the steering wheel with enough strength to crush the hard plastic. White smoke left a trail behind him. Burning rubber singed his nostrils. He looked around. No one had moved. Everyone seemed paralyzed where they were. Evan took a long breath and pushed open his door.

Before he could set foot on the ground, an angry voice said, "Have you lost your mind?"

"Rose!"

"Do you know how close you came to killing us all?" Her hand waved in the air to include all the cars in the intersection.

Evan scrambled out of the SUV's cab and grabbed Rose. "Are you all right?" He crushed her to him, suddenly realizing that the car turning right was hers. He could have killed her. The closeness of the accident, the thought that he could be the cause of hurt to her had him trembling.

In Lighthouse and most of Maine, people drove Jeeps and four-wheel-drive vehicles due to the weather. He hadn't taken a second thought when he saw the Jeep coming.

"Of course I'm all right," she said, pushing herself out of his arms. She brushed at her sleeves as if he'd covered her in dust. "You're the crazy one."

"Not entirely." Horns behind them blew a discordant symphony. Evan surveyed the haphazard way cars blocked the intersection. "We better move our cars. Thankfully, I didn't make contact with anyone."

Rose didn't argue, although her body was stiff as she headed behind his vehicle and toward her own car. He pulled himself into the driver's seat. The oncoming lane was clear and Evan maneuvered around Rose's car and continued up the street. Less than a minute later he was in his driveway. Seconds later Rose parked in hers.

"Rose, I'm sorry," he said the moment she got out of her car. "I've had a bad day and I just wanted to get home quickly."

"From the way you were driving, you could have caused a major catastrophe and we'd all be in the hospital. Just where would that leave the town?"

She was shaken. He didn't need to be a doctor to see that, although she was fighting it. He'd been trembling too. The thought of hurting Rose disturbed him. But seeing her, fighting tears, fighting to remain calm, Evan suddenly thought he needed to apologize for more than a near accident.

"I'll be more careful," he said.

The fight seemed to go out of her then. She turned away, almost snapping her attention in another direction. She went to her mailbox. Evan stood where he was next to the Belgian-stone curb that separated their two driveways.

"I suppose your bad day had to do with the lighthouse," Rose said on her return. She held several sale flyers and a couple of envelopes. Appearing to be more in control of herself after the short trip, she looked at the lighthouse on the hill above them.

"I don't suppose there is a single person in town who doesn't know I'm planning to use a color other than white on that lighthouse."

"Maybe Yvette Roberta Collins. I doubt if she knows yet, but give her a day or so."

"Who's Yvette Roberta Collins? I don't remember her."

"She was born about three hours ago—eight pounds, seven ounces, twenty-three inches long, curly black hair, blue eyes. Mother and daughter doing well. Father hyperventilated in delivery room." Rose smiled and Evan felt a yearning inside himself come to life.

"You delivered a baby today?"

"Sometimes doctors have to do that."

"At least your day was more significant than mine."

"Ever think of just painting it white?" she asked.

"Yeah…" He laughed mirthlessly. "That's what was on my mind when I went through the intersection."

"I suppose that means you're set in your ways."

He didn't like the way she said that. As if there was no room for compromise in him. He wanted to ask her where she stood on the subject, but he didn't know if he was prepared for her answer.

"I'm not set in my ways. Compromise is part of my everyday life, but when I believe in something, I *will* fight for it."

"And you believe the color of the lighthouse is something to take a stand on?"

"Not exactly."

"Then why are you doing it?"

"Nobody even asked me to just paint it white. They all attacked me, saying I couldn't do it. They made me feel like a criminal."

"Evan, you know that wasn't their intention."

"Yeah. I suppose I have been away a long time. And I talk funny. Many of the people I knew have moved away. Their younger siblings have grown up. To them I'm an outsider."

"I remember you," she said softly.

There was that shock of sensation that went through him at her words. "How about having dinner with me tonight?" Evan asked without thinking. With what he'd been through today, he needed a friendly face.

"All right." Her smile brightened. The doctor in her was gone and the woman shone through. "What time?"

Evan looked at his watch. "Say forty-five minutes from now."

"When you give a time period it's always precise."

"Occupational hazard. We're used to scheduling minute by minute."

"All right, I can do forty-five minutes."

"I thought we'd drive over to Seaverton and eat at Florham Manor. It is still there, I hope."

"It's still there. Seaverton is an hour away."

"I forgot, you have medical duties here."

"That's not it. I'll call Doc Kidd to cover for me. Why do you want to go so far?"

"I want to have a pleasant meal without anyone accosting me or even mentioning that damn lighthouse. And by the way, that means no discussion of it from you either."

"On the lighthouse, no discussion." With her hand, she imitated zipping her mouth closed. "Although some good has come from your involvement with it."

"What's that?"

She tucked her mail under her arm and took his hands in hers, holding them with their palms together. "They're no longer shaking."

Chapter 5

Florham Manor was the oldest continuously operating restaurant in northern Maine. According to the
history of the place, which was sold in a bound book
in every gift shop in the state, William MacLoren and
his wife, Maureen, arrived from Scotland in 1693.
To survive in the wilderness, Maureen began serving
food to the fishermen from a small log cabin. That
cabin became Florham Manor.

Rose didn't know if the story was true or if it
had been embellished through the years, but
everyone in Maine knew it. Tonight it didn't matter
what the history was or whether it was true or fic-

tionalized, Rose felt like a queen and nothing would mar that. With Brett being ill, they hadn't gone out much as he'd had to stick to his exercise program and diet requirements. Eating out wasn't something they could do often, especially in Boston. Had they lived in Lighthouse, she could have called Kings and discussed his menu with the cook. Evan didn't have any of those restrictions. She tucked Brett into the back of her mind. The image of Evan commandeered her thoughts.

Forty-five minutes had been sufficient when she thought they were going to Kings, but it rushed by with the speed of a gale when she had to decide what to wear to Florham Manor. From the back of her closet she'd spied the deep maroon calf-length dress she hadn't worn since her return to Lighthouse.

As the waiter led them to a table for two in the oldest part of the building, Rose smiled at the memory of Evan's face when he saw her. She'd taken her hair out of the unobtrusive ponytail and hot-curled it, allowing it to frame her face in ringlets. With a little mascara and lipstick, she finished her makeup and thanked her ancestors for the healthy, fresh-air look of her skin.

"What would you look like if I'd said I'd pick you up in an hour?" he'd asked rhetorically.

She wasn't the only one looking like they were headed to a ball. He was wearing a formal suit, what she believed was his signature white shirt and highly polished shoes. She could remember him in cutoff jeans with ragged edges and deck shoes washing his first car. While this look wasn't raw with sex like the cutoffs, it had her insides shaking as violently as his hands had when he first arrived in town.

Rose knew her eyes were as large as double moons. She felt like Cinderella at the ball. And Prince Charming was holding her arm. Evan held her chair and she sat facing the flood-lighted area outside. During the day she would have been able to see the Atlantic Ocean across the rocks.

The place was packed since this was the height of the tourist season. The trees wouldn't begin to turn for another couple of weeks, but people were already trying to get in the last few days of good weather.

Rose set her purse on the windowsill next to her and hung her pager and cell phone on the outside.

"Do you have an early call tomorrow morning?" Evan asked.

"I always have to be ready. Even though Doc Kidd is covering, there could be an emergency."

"Lighthouse needs more doctors."

She nodded. "I agree. With Doc Kidd leaving, I'll have no one to consult with when necessary. And no one to cover for me so I can have more nights like this one." Rose heard the implication of her words the moment they left her mouth. She was sorry she'd said them. She hadn't meant to imply that she expected Evan to take her out more often. Confused, she rushed on. "When I came back a year ago, the town had set up a committee to look into attracting more doctors to the area. I think they're getting pressure from the plant."

"Are there more injuries because of the plant?"

"Some," Rose said. "The plant expanded last year and it has no doctor. They have a nurse, but she's not always available."

"From what I can see," Evan said, "it's amazing that they are open to change caused by the expansion and stalwart about the lighthouse."

"I thought we weren't going to talk about the lighthouse," Rose said.

"We aren't."

The waiter came to take their dinner order and deliver the drinks they'd ordered when they sat down. When he left, Rose raised her glass and toasted Evan. "To meeting old friends."

"Friends," he said, holding his glass of ginger ale.

They drank. Rose set her glass down and leaned her arms on the table in front of her. "You don't drink, do you?"

"I used to. I was advised not to do it for a while."

"Ah," she said. "By that nonexistent doctor in the District of Columbia."

Evan took another drink. "And we're not going to talk about that either."

Rose nodded. She wouldn't push. Not tonight. Evan seemed to be coming along fine. His hands no longer shook and he was interacting with the community. Though she hadn't counted on him butting heads with the old guard over the color of the lighthouse.

He'd had all the earmarks of clinical depression when she first saw him. But his teaching school was helping. Taking his life one day at a time was good. She knew he'd survive his trauma, whatever it was. His healing had already begun.

"Rose." Evan called her back from her thoughts. His face was more serious than she expected it. A tiny precognitive fear found a crack in her heart and planted its feet in it. "The other night at Kings I was talking to Matt and Claudia…" He paused and looked down. She knew what was coming.

"They told you about Brett?"

He nodded. "I'm sorry. I didn't know."

"How could you? You haven't been here since your parents left for Egypt."

"You can tell me to stop," he said. "I haven't told you about my past. You have a right to privacy too."

Rose sipped her drink. "What did they tell you?"

"They said he died after the wedding."

"That's true."

"Why didn't you tell me?"

"For pity's sake. I didn't want it."

"Rose, I don't pity you. I think you're the bravest, strongest woman I've ever met."

"With all the women you know? You work for a U.S. senator."

"And she couldn't survive half of what you have without an entourage large enough to protect her from every conceivable crisis. You anticipate crisis and go after it."

"Thank you," was all she could think to say. After a moment she told him the whole story. "It was late in the day. We'd worked around schedules so I could get off in time to change clothes and meet Brett in the judge's chambers. The ceremony was very small. We decided to marry and made the arrangements in a week."

She glanced at Evan, wondering what he was thinking. He was her best friend and she hadn't invited him to her wedding. She'd invited no friend from Lighthouse. Everything went so fast after they decided to make it happen.

"Only a few people from the hospital were invited as witnesses," she tried to explain. "My parents made it on a moment's notice. His parents came reluctantly."

Evan raised an eyebrow but said nothing.

"We married against his family wishes. They didn't feel Brett was strong enough for marriage. Brett objected, but when he died several months later they blamed me."

"Rose, you can't blame yourself for that. You had no way of knowing."

"I know that," she said. Her mind told her that. Her friends and parents had told her that, but she still wondered if the stress of adjusting to marriage hadn't contributed to his heart attack.

Pushing the thought away, she went on. "Several months later, we went for a walk. It was part of the exercise program that had become routine. Suddenly, he grabbed his chest and my arm. It was over in seconds. I performed CPR until the ambulance arrived. The paramedics tried too, but he was gone."

She stopped, swallowing the emotions that welled up in her throat. Rose thought she could tell the story dispassionately but found all the old questions of why did she let it happen came back to accuse her.

Evan reached over and put his hand over hers. "You don't have to go on," he said.

"I'm all right. I want you to know." Squeezing her hand inside his, she continued. "With all I had learned as a doctor, there was nothing I could do to save his life."

She finished. Evan held on to her hand with both of his. "I'm so sorry, Rose. I understand how you feel."

"Thanks."

The waiter interrupted them. Evan moved his hands to allow the huge platter holding a Maine lobster to be set in front of him. Rose had Alaskan crab legs. She inhaled the delicious aroma of the food. "This smells good." Rose used the meal to change the subject and lightened the heaviness that had fallen over their table.

"I haven't had a real Maine lobster in years," Evan said.

"You should come home more often." She pulled out a fork full of crabmeat, dipped it in the butter and put it in her mouth. It tasted better than anything she'd ever eaten.

"I'm thinking of it."

"What?"

"Just for the food." His grin said he was teasing her. Rose relaxed a bit. Her pulse had jumped along with her conclusions, when she thought he might be thinking of staying in Lighthouse.

"There are a few other attractions." She looked around the room. "Look at all the tourists. The trees will peak soon."

"And there's you."

"Me?" She could barely get the word out.

"Living next door to the most beautiful woman in town has its benefits. Where else can a man find someone to talk to at three o'clock in the morning?"

"I kinda like having that house occupied too." She liked having *him* there, but she couldn't let him know it. "When you leave, have you thought of renting it? It's fully furnished and Mrs. Wormly does a good job of keeping it up. With so many new people coming to town, I'm sure she wouldn't have a problem finding tenants." Rose gave the impression that she'd like to use it as a selling point for the town. But the only person she wanted in that house was Evan.

Evan was shaking his head. "It's really not my decision. My parents still own the house. But either way, I'm not up to renting yet. Coming back, even with the town against me, has made me feel more like this is where my roots are. I need the familiar. I need to know that things are as I expect them to be. I hope you don't mind."

"Evan, I love having you next door. It was just a thought."

"I was only half kidding when I said I'm thinking of coming up more often. I might be using the house more than I have in the past."

"What about your job in Washington? Teaching at the high school and painting the lighthouse can't compare to the pace or the excitement of being one of the shapers of life in this country."

"The job has its moments, but it could be lost with the next election." He paused to take a bite of his food. "I've been thinking a lot about my life in the time I've been here."

"Oh," she said, concentrating on her food to keep from letting him see the color she could feel painting her face. "What have you decided?"

"Nothing, yet. It's hard to compare D.C. to Lighthouse. They are two different places. I love my life in the District. I'm comfortable there. I love the excitement of the city. There's almost a rhythm you can see and feel. And I do like standing on the lines of history." He took a moment to smile at her. "When the next election takes place I could be swept right onto the White House staff."

Rose noted the way his body moved when he spoke, the way he leaned forward and clenched his fists as if he was making a point, the exhilaration in his voice. All were signs of a man who truly loved what he did.

"I didn't know that."

Evan hunched a shoulder as if he were blowing off the possibility.

"It sounds like a wonderful opportunity for you." Rose hoped her words didn't sound flat. She was truly happy for Evan. He'd found what he wanted to do and was doing it. Yet somewhere in her mind, she wished things were different.

"It is," he said. "But doing it is more time consuming than what I do now."

"Do you think the stress is too much?" She was thinking of the reason he'd come back to Lighthouse.

He was shaking his head before she finished speaking. "I thrive on stress. I know you might not believe that, since you know I came here as a result of stress, but I do."

"Then what is your dilemma?" she asked.

"Being here is also appealing. I didn't know how much I missed it until I came back. I like the slower pace, the friendly atmosphere. I like knowing most of the townspeople and speaking to them on the street. That kind of thing doesn't happen in D.C. When you stop someone to speak, it's because you want something. A vote, their opinion, their position on something. Here none of that comes into play."

"Not even the lighthouse controversy?"

He smiled what Rose often diagnosed as the emotional smile. It was filled with memory, good memories of the past that came in a flash and were never explained.

"Even that," he said. "Then there's—"

"What?" she prompted when he stopped. "There's what?" As his smile faded, his stare became more intense. Rose felt as if he was looking into her mind and seeing what was in her heart.

"Evan," she called, but he didn't respond. He kept his eyes fixed on her. "Evan," she said his name again.

"What?"

"You stopped in the middle of the sentence. What were you going to say?"

"Nothing important."

Rose knew that wasn't true.

"Does it have anything to do with what brought you back to Lighthouse?"

This time there was a bit of a little-boy grin on his face. "No, it doesn't."

"Then what?"

"Are you going to nag me the rest of the night?"

"Only until you tell me what I want to know. And I am not a nag."

"No, you're a determined doctor."

"Don't change the subject."

"All right, it isn't what brought me here, but what's keeping me here."

"What's that?" She knew it couldn't be painting the lighthouse.

"A subject for another time," he told her.

Rose waited a moment, taking time to finish the

last of her crab legs. "All right. I know when I'm up against a wall. Keep your reasons to yourself."

He laughed at her frustration. Rose found it hard to be angry with him. This was the first time she felt he was really relaxed, that whatever trauma he'd sustained, he was dealing with it or he'd conquered it.

"If you won't tell me your reasons for staying here, why don't you tell me what it's like to work for a senator."

"She's very much in demand. She speaks at universities, press clubs, organizational events and the floor of Congress. She's on several very important committees. I have to do as much research as I do writing, even though there are researchers on staff. I have to anticipate what the press will ask her so she can have well-crafted answers ready and she doesn't come across as uninformed or create a situation that requires damage control."

"It sounds very important."

He stopped eating and gazed at her. "A lot of it is public relations. I'm one of the background players, making sure everything goes as planned. With the number of lobbyists in D.C., it takes a lot of effort."

Rose enjoyed hearing him talk. He obviously was a connective part of the Washington machine and thrived on being part of the mechanism. They finished dinner and moved to the small lounge connected to the restaurant. There was live music and dancing. Rose relished being in Evan's arms again without the need to subdue her feelings.

She didn't know how much time went by as they danced. One song blended into another and Evan kept her in his arms. She closed her eyes and floated away, with the music lifting her feet, the smell of his cologne creating fantasies in her mind and the feel of his arms holding her as if she belonged next to his heart.

When they finally realized the time and left, Rose was sorry the night had to end. The drive back to Lighthouse was mostly silent, but it had a warm, velvet feel to it. Two friends who understood each other, knew secrets and didn't need to fill the air with voice.

Evan pulled in to his driveway and turned the engine off. The small cabin was filled with a different silence, a reluctant silence. Rose didn't want to pierce the fantasy of the evening. It had been as near to perfect as she could get. Evan got out and came around to her side. He opened the door and the cold night air rushed in. She got out and with his arm around her waist, he walked her through the gate and along the walkway to her front door.

"Thank you," Evan said.

She turned and looked up at him. "For what?"

"For keeping your promise not to discuss the lighthouse. For telling me about Brett. For dancing my feet off."

The both laughed.

"And for being one of the reasons I'd want to stay here."

Rose's head came up quickly, her eyes widening as she refused to believe she could have heard him correctly. Her throat closed before she could utter a word. Evan's head bent and his lips touched hers. She'd wanted him to kiss her. She'd thought about it, dreamed of it, but inside her was a measure of self-preservation. She moved to step away. Evan's arms caught her around the waist and pulled her back. Rose lost control of the purse in her hand. She ignored the thud it made as it hit the bricks near her feet. Her hands slid up Evan's chest and around his neck. She leaned into him. His arms encircled her, tightly fitting her body into his.

His mouth worked magic on hers. As the light spun over the town, she knew that all the walls she'd built around her heart, to keep from feeling, to hold in the misery that left her empty and alone, to keep her safe from hurt, burst with Evan's mouth making contact with hers.

Warmth poured over her, blocking out the crisp nature of the night air. Evan's hands moved back, spanning her waist. Then they rolled over her curves, reaching her hips and sending spirals of sensation through her from her toes to the core of her being. He lifted his head for a moment, nudged her back and looked into her eyes. Then he repositioned his mouth over hers.

The change in placement also changed the depth of the kiss. Rose was crushed against Evan. The ghosts of her past melted away, leaving her free and alive. She pressed herself into Evan's body as if the two of them were merging into one. His mouth skated across hers, his tongue invading space reserved for him. Rose went up on her toes. She clung to him. One foot came off the ground and she balanced herself against him. Her body, toned from a practiced exercise program, felt soft as it pressed into the hard contours of his. His arms came back to her waist, holding her tight while streams of passion flowed through her.

Finally, out of breath, Evan raise his head. Rose rested against him. She hadn't expected to feel like this, to be so completely involved—body, mind and spirit. So in tune with Evan.

"You better go in now," Evan said. His voice was husky, almost hoarse. Rose knew he'd been deeply affected by the kiss. Pushing herself back, she hoped he couldn't tell by looking at her how hard her heart was beating, how profoundly things within her had changed.

She opened the door and stepped inside, turning to look at him. Evan hunkered down and retrieved her purse. He handed it to her, then reached up and ran his hand down the side of her face.

"See you soon."

Rose nodded, incapable of speech. She closed the door and leaned against it, licking her lips, tasting Evan. She held it, willing it to stay in place, willing it to remain with her for at least the rest of the night.

The door closed and Evan stood there a moment watching the cyclic light play on the door glass. It had played on Rose's face too, winking in and out, giving him only a promise of things to be. When he turned he saluted the lighthouse, no longer looking at it as the symbol of contention that had prompted the evening.

He walked down the steps and through the fence. The night had been revealing. Rose had told him about Brett. She'd put them back on the footing they'd had when they lived next door to each other and she represented the sister he'd never had. But he didn't want her as a sister anymore. From the way she responded to his kiss, she wasn't looking for the brother in him either.

Whistling the last song they had danced to, he slipped his hands into his pockets and sauntered around their cars. Taking the three steps to his porch in one giant lunge, he totally twisted in the air, coming down hard on the wooden floor, almost in one fluid movement. Then he stopped, sobered, his chest pumping up and down as he saw the paper tacked above the door knocker. Someone wanted to make sure he got it, Evan thought. They'd pinned it to the door like an eviction notice.

Snapping it free, he read the front cover. It was folded like a subpoena. The revolving light made the words flash at him. Certain of them, like *town meeting,* jumped blindingly off the paper. The message stated a meeting had been called for a week from today in the high-school auditorium. A vote would be taken on the color of the lighthouse.

"Damn," Evan cursed. He slapped the paper over his hand. His good mood was gone. He'd returned to Lighthouse and to reality. Anger welled up in him.

"Well, if it's a fight you want," he said to the paper, "you've come to the right man."

There wasn't a free seat in the auditorium. The noise level was high and heated. A dais had been set up and name tents identified where everyone should sit. Evan's name was aptly placed on the end and to the left, as the audience would face it. Life in Washington crept into his thinking and he wondered if that had been done on purpose. The five council members were all on stage, although they weren't seated. They appeared to be caucusing in a group upstage. Evan was on the floor. He smiled, shook hands and exchanged pleasantries with old friends, introduced himself to strangers and reacquainted himself with people who had been too young to vote when he left.

He tried to read the crowd. Evan knew that the people who generally attended meetings were the ones who had a grievance. Supporters weren't often the majority in attendance. The average age was heavily favoring older citizens. He also knew these were the people who most wanted to keep the status quo. *If it ain't broke, don't fix it* could have been tattooed on their foreheads.

The one friendly face he didn't see was Rose's. They hadn't connected for most of the week. Their comings and goings were like playing car tag. When he was home, she wasn't. He'd wanted to continue what they started on her doorstep, but with only a week to prepare for this meeting, he hadn't had the chance.

"I think we should get started." Jeff Altman banged the gavel on the table and the room settled down. Evan made his way to the stage, walking up the side steps on the right and all the way across the stage to his seat. Every eye in the place was on him and he made sure to make eye contact with different council members as he trekked to his assigned station.

When he was seated, Jeff cleared his throat and began. "You all know why we're here."

There was general nodding from the audience as if he'd begun a call-and-response sermon in morning service.

"The lighthouse has provided safe passage…" Jeff launched into a speech on the history of the lighthouse that went on for twenty-five minutes. Evan kept his face straight and tried to appear interested in what was being said. He'd known Jeff would do this and expected the same from the other council members.

He wasn't disappointed. Two hours after they'd begun, the third council member went to the podium and spoke on the traditions of New Englanders. Evan watched the body language. People were tired, fidgeting in their chairs, and a few openly yawned. He'd been counting on this. Wanting to smile, he stifled it, instead forcing himself to appear attentive to the speaker giving information they'd all learned in civics class in this high school. With the lighthouse revolving since each of them had been born and with tourists invading the small town to view the lighthouse, it was difficult not to always have the facts of tradition at your fingertips. In truth, no one had given a good reason to keep the lighthouse the same color. They'd offered plenty of rhetoric. Evan would have no problem standing any one of the council members up against the best congressional orators.

Finally, Jeff Altman returned to the podium and introduced Evan. He walked to the podium carrying nothing. He had no notes, no clipboard, no sheafs of paper. Everything he wanted to say would appear to come from his heart. That was his appeal. It wasn't practiced speeches or researched material gathered in readiness for this meeting, although he was ready and he'd done plenty of research. But he knew the best speeches were the ones that touched the audience, that transported them from their seats in a sea of us versus them, to the stage where they were part of the action, part of the decision making.

Evan resisted the urge to turn to Jeff and smile. The councilman had no idea what was in store for him. Evan was an expert at the art of persuasion, and he was about to paint a picture worthy of the masters.

Chapter 6

"Good evening," he began. "I'm not going to make a speech tonight. I just want to talk to you." He leaned across the podium and adjusted the microphone. Then walked away from it. He noticed the commotion in the audience. They were probably wondering what he was doing.

He walked in front of the dais and when he reached the podium, he took the microphone in his hand and said, "Since I'm not going to make a speech, I feel standing behind that—" he glanced at the podium "—is too formal." It was a tactic that brought him closer to the audience, and instinctively they perked up as if he was going to tell them a secret. "Actually, before I begin, it's a little warm in here. Do you mind if I take off my jacket?" A general stirring gave him permission. "In fact, anybody out there who wants to take off his jacket or stand up and stretch go right ahead. We've been sitting a long time."

Relief sounded through the auditorium as people complied. Rose slipped into the back of the room then. She wore a red parka and had pulled her hair free of the standard ponytail. She made eye contact with him and he smiled. He was relieved to see her. After a week of only glancing at her from a distance, checking her empty driveway and missing her more than he thought possible, he felt a surge of warmth.

"Everybody comfortable?" This time the atmosphere seemed a little more relaxed. "In the interest of time, let's get right to the matter at heart. We all know the history of the lighthouse. What you might not know is that the lighthouse hasn't always been white." He paused, waiting for general dissent and he wasn't disappointed.

At the back of the room he checked Rose's position. She hadn't moved. He tried to determine what she was thinking but couldn't.

"Colleen," Evan called.

From behind him, the stage curtain was

pulled apart by two hands and one of his students walked out carrying a huge easel with a poster on it. The people at the dais twisted around to see.

"The first settlers to this area built a wooden lighthouse on the same plot where later the one we know would stand."

The room strained to see the poster. "For those of you who can't see, check the large screens on either side of the stage." On cue, two screens, Evan had seen hung that afternoon, simultaneously showed a huge replication of the poster.

"This was in the early 1700s. As Jeff told you, the current structure was built in 1830."

"The paint is gray," Evan said in a strong voice. "Apparently, they ran out of paint three-quarters of the way up and used a separate color for the remainder."

Evan acknowledged the librarian sitting in the front row. She'd provided him with the information. "In 1837 there was a huge storm that came down the coast. It damaged the lighthouse." Another student came out from the curtain with a photo of the damaged wooden structure. At the same time, the screens produced a replica.

Evan heard gasps as if the gathering had lived through the storm and understood how it affected the inhabitants of the tiny coastal village.

"When the structure was repaired, it was painted yet another color."

The expectation of a student walking through the stage-curtain and the screens producing an image had the audience immediately training their gazes on those areas of the room. Jim Wiley, from Evan's fifth-period class, carried the posterboard. The image on the screens came up in black and white, but Jim's reproduction had been painted.

"What color was it painted, Jim?" Evan asked in his teacher voice.

Wearing a body microphone, Jim's voice could be heard through the auditorium. "The bottom was stripes of red and white and the top was blue."

"In truth, the lighthouse wasn't painted white until 1915. The thought was that warplanes might infiltrate the U.S. and could use the lighthouse as a landmark. Since the light revolves once every three seconds, painting it white seems like a moot point." The audience laughed.

"That was almost a hundred years ago, Evan," a white-haired man from the audience called out. "And in Maine, that's a tradition."

The room laughed again. Evan joined them.

"That's true, sir." Evan was sure the man had once served in the armed forces and Evan's pronunciation of the word *sir* was a salute. "It seems this assembly would like the lighthouse painted white and I'm willing to acquiesce to your wishes and follow the *Maine tradition.*"

Thunderous applause broke out in the room. The town council was smiling and patting themselves on the back. They had won. Evan waited. He wasn't finished yet. He raised his arms for the room to quiet.

"However, Jeff has said that we would take a vote, so we need to follow protocol."

"And that's a Maine tradition too," the same old man shouted. Again there was laughter. The man couldn't know that he was providing much-needed relief for the room.

And playing right into Evan's hands.

"To vote, you need something to vote for and against." Without giving anyone a chance to argue with him, Evan continued, "Here are your options."

The curtains behind him opened. The back doors of the auditorium opened. In came students, each carrying one of three different color combinations and designs for the lighthouse.

The room erupted in confusion, discussion and general noise. Evan made no attempt to calm it. He watched as people discussed their preferences, picked out the colors they liked best, determined the ones most pleasing to the eye.

After a moment, Jeff began banging the gavel

and calling for order in the room. It took a while for them to quiet down.

Evan hadn't relinquished the floor and had no intention of doing so. At his signal the students began passing papers out.

"As you can see," Evan said, "ballots are being passed out. With the council's permission, we can use these to vote on the design and colors of your choice."

He looked at the council. Jeff was sputtering. Veins popped out on his head and he could hardly speak. Twenty minutes later, ballots had been marked and were busily being counted by a committee of leading citizens.

The results were handed to Jeff and he looked at them as he stood up. Evan didn't move.

Clearing his throat, Jeff spoke into the microphone. "The design receiving the most votes is number three." The room erupted in applause, drowning out Jeff's voice as he stated the design's characteristics.

No one waited for the meeting to be adjourned. People stood up and began talking in groups, some shaking hands, some gathering jackets and sweaters to leave. Many approached the stage to congratulate Evan.

Rose stood in place, never once having moved from her spot. There was no expression on her

face. She hadn't smiled or commented. Evan
realized she'd never given him which side of the
argument she was on. When they'd had dinner,
the subject was off limits. Now he wondered.
Several people spoke to her and she responded,
giving them the replies they expected, since no one
looked at her as if they disagreed with what she
said.

"Well, Evan, if you can live with red and white,
I can too." Jeff Altman stuck his hand out and
Evan took it.

"Thanks, Jeff."

The entire council shook his hand as they filed
out. That was one of the things he loved about
Lighthouse; people could disagree with you, but
eventually they all took it in stride and pitched in.

It took a while for him to finish shaking hands
and make his way to the back of the room. Rose
pushed herself away from the wall and walked
toward him. He could tell by her body language
that where they had been a week ago on her
doorstep was light-years away from where they
were tonight.

"You must be happy," she said. "You won."

Evan pushed his hands deep into his pockets.
"Yes, I won." His voice was flat. Rose could inter-
pret that as him being tired. She gave no indication
that she thought of it one way or another. Evan was

used to reading nonverbal communication. He prided himself on it. It helped him determine how he could advise the senator. Thankfully Rose lived and worked in Lighthouse, because she was an enigma to him. If she were a lobbyist, an aide, or even a member of Congress, he'd have a difficult time reading what she was saying beyond her words.

"You never said where you stood on the issue," Evan said.

"A week ago, I was for leaving it the same color."

"And now?"

"I agree with the town. I like the designs. They're dramatic, beautifully detailed and excellently presented."

"You were persuaded by my argument?"

"Oh, your presentation was impressive."

"But…"

"Is this what you do in Washington? Convince people of things they don't want? Project it up on thirty-foot screens in living color, with sight and sound and dramatic effect?" Her arms waved to illustrate her point.

Evan stood up straighter. He didn't like her characterization. "Sometimes," he said. "Sometimes you have to protect people, even from themselves."

"Come on, Evan, you can't really believe the color of the lighthouse is protecting anyone."

"I was only making a point."

"Well, what is it?" she asked. "Because I don't get it."

"That just because we've done things one way for a century doesn't mean change isn't good."

Rose stared at him. He couldn't tell if she believed him or not.

"Where'd those screens come from?" she finally asked.

"Special order. The students and I spent all day setting them up. I'm donating them to the school."

"And that makes it all right?"

She turned away. Evan caught her arm. She stopped but didn't turn back to him. Her gaze was trained on the floor. "Rose, what's wrong?"

"Nothing," she said. With that she snapped her arm free of his hand and walked out the door.

Evan didn't follow her. He sat down in the last row and stared at the empty room. The projectors were all off, but the debris of the meeting was scattered about. The huge posters he'd had made in Seaverton sat in the positions where the students had left them.

Rose had said it for him, but he knew the truth. He didn't feel good about what he'd done. He'd manipulated a crowd. Not for a noble purpose or one he believed in with his heart and soul, but one that only allowed him to have his way. He felt like a thief. This was not what he did in Washington. When he wrote a speech for Senator DeLong, it was based on facts that meant something. It relieved pain, made life better for thousands, if not millions, of people.

Tonight, he'd only proved that his classes in persuasive speeches had paid off. He'd robbed the town of their tradition.

But more important, he'd lost Rose's respect.

The first thing Evan noticed when he pulled in to his driveway and got out of the SUV was that the scaffolding had begun to go up on the light-house. The second thing was that Rose's car was parked in the usual place but her house was completely dark. He wondered if she was still stewing or if the tongue-lashing she'd given him at the high school had expunged her anger.

He took a step toward her house and stopped, deciding to give her time. Both of them probably needed to calm down. And living next door to each other, how long could she avoid him?

Evan went inside, but found himself restless. He should be out celebrating. It's what he would have done if he were still in the District. Thinking of that, he went to his computer and checked e-mail. There were nearly a thousand messages waiting for him. It took him three hours and several beers to get through them. He hadn't had a beer in three months, since he'd trashed his office. Mrs. Wormly knew his taste and when she stocked the refrigerator, she included his favorite brand. So far he had resisted them in favor of ginger ale, orange juice or bottled water. But tonight he reached for the long-neck bottle and downed the first one in two long swigs.

Most of the messages were to keep him informed or asking how he was doing. There were a few he answered, sending a report saying the vacation was doing him good and he expected to return on time. He answered a few questions, made some suggestions for speeches the senator had on her calendar, edited a speech sent to him for comment and signed off.

Closing the lid of the laptop at 2:00 a.m., Evan was wide awake. His head buzzed a bit from the beer, but sleeping was not on his mind. Rose occupied that space. Taking his parka from the hook by the kitchen door, he left the house and walked up to the lighthouse. The wind spit at him, whipping the parka back with its force.

The scaffolding circled the base, rising to about six feet. He knew that was a pattern. Every six feet there would be a platform to stand on and paint the space from one rung to the next. He opened the door that led through the mudroom to the spiral staircase that rose clockwise to the lamp room and gallery where the Fresnel lens cast light upon the water. Going up the steps, he circled around and around until he came onto the platform that looked out on the town and the sea.

The sky was overcast tonight, but with the light turning he wouldn't be able to see the stars at this range anyway. Below him the town slept. He could make out the high school and the church steeple of the oldest church in Lighthouse. He saw his house and Rose's. Out to sea, the dark water hit the rocky coast. Evan leaned against the window ledge and watched it. After a moment he was no longer seeing the surface. His mind was back to the restaurant, to Rose in his arms on her doorstep, to tonight when she'd looked at him as if he were the enemy.

Evan stood up and shrugged out of his parka. It was warm in the tower and he'd probably be here for a while. Something hit the floor. He looked down to see the baby rattle. Reaching down, he picked it up. Gabe's rattle. He hadn't thought of Gabe in days. He'd been so focused on the meeting, and Rose, that everything else had gone out of his head.

Even his son.

What kind of father was he? How could he forget his own son? He fingered the silver rattle. He'd bought it the day after Alana told him she was pregnant. He'd been so happy. His own home life had been adventurous and wonderful. He looked forward to sharing the same kind of things with his own child. It hadn't mattered whether it was a boy or girl. There were hundreds of things he could do with a son or a daughter. But he'd gotten a boy, a son. Then fate had stepped in, ripping his future away.

The fire had come, taking all his plans for future trips, ball games, circus clowns, tossing balls in the backyard and destroyed them. Snuffed them out like the north wind blowing down from the coast.

Evan crushed the rattle in his hand. He squeezed his eyes shut at the loss that moved through him, creating a void in his life. But, for the first time, instead of seeing only the red flames of the fire in his mind, Rose's face appeared; soft, warm and smiling. Evan didn't feel lost. He felt as if he'd found something he didn't know he needed. Yet it was out of reach.

He needed to do something about that.

Making a quick decision, he grabbed his parka and took a step toward the stairs. Then he saw her.

"Rose!"

"Sooner or later, one of us has got to get some sleep," Rose said. She stepped onto the platform.

Evan frowned. "What are you doing here?"

"I came to see if you were all right."

Evan slipped his hand in his pocket and dropped the rattle. Bringing his hands out again, he held both of them in front of Rose.

"I thought you would never talk to me again."

"I'm only here as a doctor," she said flatly.

"So you are still angry with me?"

Rose turned around. In a moment she'd start down the stairs again. "No shakes, Doctor."

She turned back, glancing at his hands and then up at him. His hands might be steady, but she had rocked the rest of him with her appearing out of the silence as if he'd conjured her up in his mind, Evan wanted to take her in his arms, but he wanted Rose, the woman. And he was looking at Rose, the doctor. Even though she might be angry with him, she was bound to look after his welfare.

"Just checking." She turned to go down the steps.

"Rose," Evan called her name. She stopped and faced him. "Please, don't go. I can't remember a time when we were angry with each other. Peace?"

She walked past him and put her hands on the ledge where he'd been leaning. "It's a nice night for stargazing."

He stood next to her, close enough to feel the heat of her body and aware of his own escalating temperature.

"When I was little I used to think I could see Europe from here."

"You would need an extremely clear day." Evan tried to lighten the mood, but Rose's face remained straight.

"And the ability to see over the curvature of the earth." She laughed then. "But when you're young anything is possible. I could see myself sitting in an outdoor café drinking wine and eating fruit and cheese." The humor was gone. She sounded regretful.

"Did you ever go?"

"To Paris?" She shook her head. "It was med school and then back here. What about you?"

"A couple of times. Once when I was going to visit my parents in Egypt. Once on my own." During the long flight to Egypt, he'd had a layover in Paris. His parents surprised him by meeting his plane. They spent a few days visiting the City of Light before continuing to Cairo. "You'd like it. It's everything you dreamed it is."

"Maybe one day." Her expression changed. She turned her face away so Evan couldn't see it, but before she went back to looking through the windows, he thought he saw a sadness there. The same sadness he'd noticed on Final Day.

"Rose, you asked if I was all right. How are you?"

"Me? I'm fine."

"Are you? You don't sleep." She turned to deny

it, but Evan stopped her. "You know when I'm up. It's after two in the morning now and you're still awake."

"I don't need a lot of sleep."

"I recognize that argument. I've used it myself. And you want to know what it resulted in?"

"What?"

Evan realized he'd said more than he intended. She was the doctor again. "Let's just say, it's what brought me back here."

"Did you have a nervous breakdown?"

He shook his head. "I don't know why they call it that. I wasn't nervous. Something happened. I can't even remember what it was. When I came back to reality three men were holding my arms and my office was trashed."

"And you don't remember doing it?"

He shook his head. "That doctor you wanted information on is a psychotherapist. He suggested I take some time off. The senator agreed and here I am, causing trouble in this town."

"Do you want me to contact the doctor and—"

"No," he stopped her. "We talk by videophone once a week. And you'll be happy to know he asked me if I wanted him to contact you."

"You told him about me?"

"I told him you were pushy and nosy and won't leave me to my own devices."

This brought a smile to her lips and eyes. Evan didn't tell him that he, Evan, was the one who couldn't be objective in the doctor-patient relationship.

"I don't mean to be pushy, but I take it to heart when someone needs help."

"I know." Evan raised his hand and drew it down her cheek. He couldn't resist touching her. Rose's hand came up and covered his. He stepped closer to her. "This is why you can't be my doctor." He slipped his hand around the back of her neck and drew her closer. Their mouths were close but not touching, yet they shared the air between them.

Evan touched her lips with his tongue, outlining her mouth. He felt her tremble, felt the hunger in her as her hands went to his waist and their bodies aligned with the undulating light and the universe beyond. All ten of her fingers spread out as individual digits and danced around his torso in a slow waltz. Evan pushed both his hands into her hair and seared her mouth to his.

Suddenly, he was possessed by a hunger he couldn't contain. He drew her soft body to his, melding their mouths together, holding her so tight not even air could get between them. He opened his legs, settling her into the juncture between them, and feeling a fire ignite in his veins. His mouth devoured hers. She clung to him, her arms arched to his shoulders. Their heads bobbed and weaved as one kiss led to another. Their mouths, wet, hot, hungry, demanding of each other, seeking the pleasure each could give.

Evan never thought he could feel this much sensation. Waves of it bounded through him. Rose took him to dizzying heights. The need to breathe forced him to slide his mouth from hers. The two collapsed into each other, supporting each other with their weight. Their breathing was heavy in the quiet space. Evan's chest heaved as he inhaled. He felt they were sucking in all the oxygen in the lighthouse.

Rose's hands traveled slowly up and down his back, their sensual motion keeping his body at fever pitch.

After a moment she pushed back and looked at him. "I think it's time we went to bed."

Chapter 7

The pulse of the District of Columbia was like no other city in the world. New York City was bright and flashy, fast and fun. Philadelphia was a contrast of the Old World, dwarfed by skyscrapers, and a straight run to the top of the *Rocky* stairs at the Philadelphia Museum of Art. Los Angeles was freeway and free jack, but D.C. was loaded with adrenaline. It was an all-nighter town, its illumination hidden in windowless war rooms behind heavily draped windows. Evan felt the energy of it begin to pump through his system the moment he picked up the phone.

"Senator, good morning." Evan kicked his covers off and pushed his feet to the floor. It was only seven o'clock, but Senator Katherine DeLong was an early riser.

"I wasn't sure I should call," she said. "I wanted to see how you were doing."

"I'm well," Evan said. He stifled a yawn. Usually he would have been at work for two hours by this time, but he'd been up most of the night, and life in Lighthouse didn't run on the same clocks as it did in D.C. "I'll be returning as planned."

"I'm not calling for that," she said. "It's been a while and I wanted to say hello."

Evan believed her. She was genuinely concerned about people. He enjoyed working for her because not only did she believe what she said, but she was passionate about making life better for Americans.

"I like being home. There are differences here that I don't remember, although some of the people are the same." He thought of Rose.

"Anyone special?"

Evan nearly gulped. She'd never asked him about his love life before. He supposed she hadn't had to. In D.C. his life was his work. He and Alana had been married and divorced in only two years. After he took custody of Gabe, there was no time for women other than his fifty-year-old housekeeper cum babysitter. But Rose's face immediately flew into his mind. Was she special?

"No one special," he replied. He didn't want to go there. It would lead to a conversation Evan wasn't ready to have. He wanted Rose. He knew that from holding her in his arms in the lighthouse. The remainder of the night had been worse than the former. Except for the interlude in the lighthouse, it had been a nearly dreadful end to the day. Evan had tossed and turned until the sun burned away the revolving clips of light that flashed about the walls in a rhythm as distinctive as Morse code. Rose's comment about going to bed had completely unhinged him. On the heels of her words came fantasies of them naked, entwined in each other, connected in the most intimate way, their naked bodies satiated after a night of lovemaking. But Rose had really meant getting some sleep. They were both tired. It had been a long day. Yet the night's rest eluded Evan.

"Evan, are you still there?"

The senator's voice brought him back to his surroundings. He could hear street noise in the background. "I'm here. Where are you? I hear horns blowing."

"I'm walking."

"Walking? Where?"

"Up to the Hill. I do it every day now. Since you left I've lost six pounds."

Katherine didn't really need to lose weight. She wasn't model thin, just the normal American variety of overweightness. At five foot eleven inches, her height camouflaged the extra pounds.

"If I'm going to champion health care in America, I need to practice it myself."

"So you're doing this for your health?"

"I haven't changed anything else except walking. I have even more energy than I had before."

Evan laughed. "I suppose the staff loves that." He heard the gentle fall of her laughter. It reminded him of her midwestern roots. She laughed robustly, without reservation. Yet if she were attending a formal party for a king or queen, she could easily slip into the American royalty stance and no one could find an insincere touch to her actions.

"What about you? Are you taking care of yourself?"

So she *was* calling to make sure he was all right. "I still jog every day and I'm about to embark on a painting job."

"What?"

"I'm going to paint the town's lighthouse."

"I have no doubt you'll be good at it. Just don't fall off a ladder and break anything."

"I won't."

"Gotta run now," she said. "I can see Senator Archer heading my way."

"I'll see you in a month," Evan said.

"A month? What about the ambassador's reception? You know that can help your career. And I'd like to see you there."

"I'll think about it."

They hung up then and Evan headed for his shower. The conversation with Katherine had been short, but she'd asked him a question that bugged him.

Was Rose special?

She was the first person he thought of each morning. When he'd seen her Jeep turn in to her driveway, the thought of going over and spending time with her was almost undeniably strong. His heart beat faster when she walked into a room or when she stood under the beaming circle of the light.

Yes, Rose was special.

Rose sat in her office taking a breather between patients. With both hands, she felt the heat of her face. Her skin burned every time she thought of Evan and the way he'd kissed her in the lighthouse. Brett's face smiled at her from the desk photograph. She'd taken the photo in the park where they'd met. When she looked at it now, she could see how ill he really was. His face was pale and gaunt, and his eyes were deep sockets, yet his smile was happy and beautiful.

"What do you think, Brett?" She picked up the silver frame and ran her fingers lovingly across his face. "I know you told me if anything ever happened to you, I was to go on. I've tried." Tears misted in her eyes, but she blinked them away.

The tears weren't for Brett. Rose had cried enough of those to fill a swimming pool. They weren't out of guilt either—more for a future that had been taken from them.

"You have a future," Brett had told her the day they agreed to marry. He must have known all along, Rose thought. He must have known their time would be short and that he wanted her to know she had to live without him. She hadn't wanted to, but when she found herself falling into depression, she'd remember Brett's laugh and his words.

Being with Evan had made her feel alive. She wanted to be in his arms. They were friends, good friends. They'd been that way almost their entire lives. But no more. Not after last night. They'd stepped way over the line that separated friendship from…what? They weren't lovers. At least not yet. But if judging by the way Evan had looked at her when she said they should go to bed, he was thinking of crossing to the next threshold. And Rose had gone there with him. At least in her mind.

She smiled at the thought. The smile quickly turned to a yawn. She should have gotten some sleep last night, but sleep didn't come to her easily on the best nights. And last night thoughts of Evan had replaced sleep.

Looking down, she saw she was still holding the picture frame. She should be thinking about her next patient. Rose reached to put the frame back, then changed her mind. She opened a desk drawer and slipped it inside. Slowly she closed the door. Brett's image was obscured like a curtain closing. She kept her hand on the drawer handle. She knew a curtain *had* closed on that part of her life. Evan had returned and shown her there was part of her that survived. Part of her that needed—wanted— people.

He was no longer a permanent resident of Lighthouse. He'd been definite about the amount of time he was here for. Rose would be crazy to get involved with someone who couldn't offer her the stability she craved. Lighthouse was her home. She wouldn't leave it again.

"Dr. Albright, Mrs. Maloney is waiting in room A."

Rose's head jerked up. She didn't know how

long she'd been sitting here. "Thank you," she told the nurse.

With one final look at the drawer, she removed her hand and stood up.

Maybe she *was* crazy, she thought. Her face burned again. It was already too late to change what had happened in the lighthouse.

Or how she felt about Evan.

"What are you doing?" Rose craned her neck to look up at Evan, several hours later. He was wearing a new white painter's coverall and standing inside the scaffolding at the lighthouse. He had a black baseball cap on his head with the initials FBI in white on it.

"I'm painting the lighthouse."

"I can see that. Why is it white? None of your designs have white at the bottom. At least not totally."

"This could be a primer."

She picked up the paint can, lifting it high enough for him to see the label. "But it isn't."

Evan only raised an eyebrow and went back to rolling paint on the building's surface.

"I'm glad you came by," Evan said after a moment. He didn't look at her but continued his task.

"Why?"

"I wanted to talk to you about last night."

Rose stiffened. She never thought she'd hear those words. *About last night.* What about it? It had been fireworks for her, forced her to look at her life, to examine how she would go on now that the hurt of Brett's death had been relegated to a place where she could view it without reliving it.

"I want to apologize," Evan said.

"Apologize for what?" She could barely get the words out.

"For last night. For what I did at the town meeting. Like you said, I manipulated the situation. I made this a competition, like I do in Washington. It was almost instinctual. I didn't even consider the town's true feelings. It was the need to win. I had to win and I did it using all the skills I had."

Rose let her breath out slowly. He wasn't apologizing for kissing her. Her shoulders dropped in relief that it was only the town he was apologizing about and not the change in their relationship.

"So you're painting the lighthouse white as an apology?" she asked.

"Not exactly. I intended to paint it one of the designs that I'd come up with. But the more I thought about it, the more I realized that there's comfort in returning home with the assurance that things are exactly as they were when you left them. Even if you were only gone for a few hours."

"Then why did you let it go as far as a town meeting?"

"Ego."

"What?" She took a step backward as if the solitary word had enough force to move body mass.

"Jeff Altman got to me. He never asked my intention, just assumed I was in the wrong."

"So you needed to prove your point?"

"Something like that. I never thought he'd really call a town meeting, but when the machine started to turn, there was no way of stopping it."

"Why didn't you say something at the meeting?"

"I fully intended to. But you were there. You heard the speeches. I wanted to prove to the council that there are changes going on in Lighthouse and that they aren't necessarily bad. Maybe they'll review the need for more doctors in town and a real hospital." He paused, staring intently at her. "Anyway, they want the lighthouse white. I'll give them what they want."

"So what you really learned was something about yourself?"

Evan smiled. "You know, you're another one of the things about Lighthouse that never changes."

Rose didn't know how to take that. She had changed. She was a vastly different person than the one who'd been Evan's friend nine years ago. "How do you mean that?" she asked.

"You could always see right through me."

"I don't think so. We're not the same people we were years ago, Evan. Much about our lives has changed. When we met on that bridge, the two of us were only friendly strangers. We're both holding on to experiences that have driven us along different roads."

"But at the core, we're still the same people, with the same value systems, the same dreams and hopes."

"No, Evan, that's where you're wrong. We don't have the same dreams. Life has taught us what's within our own personal realm. What we can and cannot do."

Evan put his roller down and came closer to her. "You couldn't help Brett."

She nodded her head, agreeing with him.

"What about Yvette Roberta Collins?" The two of them stood in the shadow of the mammoth tower. "Would she be alive if you weren't here to help her?"

"You're not going to play Jimmy Stewart on me and take me down the road of *It's a Wonderful Life*, are you?"

"It's not Jimmy Stewart but the angel who lets him see what life would be like without his influence. You should dwell on that during those nights when you can't sleep."

Rose peered at him as if he had the ability to look into her mind.

"You're not the only one who notices lights burning in the night," Evan said.

A weakness slipped over Rose. She felt the weight of the rock she carried on her shoulders. Sitting down on the scaffolding next to him, she laced her fingers between her legs.

"I have a problem sleeping," she admitted. "Since Brett died, I haven't had a really good night's sleep. I thought if I came home, back to familiar surroundings, things would change. But they haven't."

Evan put his arm around her and pulled her head to his shoulder. "I understand," he told her.

She relaxed against him. He was probably the only person in town who understood her circumstances. His situation was different from hers, but he had returned to Lighthouse to put his own demons behind him. Rose had returned under what she analyzed as the safety factor; at least she perceived it as that. Coming home was her haven, a place where people knew and accepted her, understood her. But it was also a place where she could hide and lick her wounds until they were scabbed over and healed.

"Time will help, Rose. I believe that," Evan said.

"Is that what people told you?"

He nodded. "All the platitudes, but the reason they say them is because they are true."

"I didn't expect it to take this long. I thought I'd be back to normal by now."

"Everyone grieves differently. You need to take care of you instead to trying to fix everyone else."

"Is that what I'm doing?" She turned her head and looked up at him.

"Isn't that the reason you stopped on the bridge?"

She waited a long moment, staring into his eyes. "I suppose it had something to do with it. I haven't analyzed it, but I *am* a doctor. Initially, I thought you were a jumper. Then I saw the D.C. tags and I recognized you."

"I had no intention of jumping from the bridge. I wouldn't need to come to Lighthouse for that. We have plenty of bridges in D.C."

"So you're going to paint this as therapy for whatever your problem is?" She indicated the lighthouse.

"It seemed like a good idea at the time."

Rose smiled. "Need any help?"

In Washington, D.C., Evan's life was chaotic, quick, a do-it-yesterday mode of living. He never thought having a daily routine could be satisfying. Yet each day he got up and went to school and interacted with his students, who never had the same questions or the same comments. Leaving school he would go to the lighthouse and paint. Rose would join him after her last patient.

He found himself searching for her, listening for the sound of her Jeep and noticing his heart speed up when she emerged into view. Darkness came earlier and they didn't have much time to paint together, yet Evan liked having her company. Even the lights, which he'd talked Mr. Wanger into hanging on the scaffolding, weren't enough to allow them to work long past sundown.

"Sorry I'm late," Rose said as she climbed the ladder. She pulled the zipper of her coveralls higher. Evan could tell she wore a jacket under it. They exchanged pleasantries about the day as they went through the vacuous motions of rolling the paint over the lighthouse's surface.

Evan noticed a change in Rose tonight. She wasn't as talkative. Her voice didn't hold as much life as it usually did. For a long while they worked in silence, Evan painting in one area, Rose in the other. Usually the two worked in unison, moving together as they rounded the building. Tonight, it was apparent that something more than physical distance separated them.

At least to Evan it was.

"It's too dark to paint anymore today," Evan shouted against the wind about an hour after she'd arrived. They'd been painting on the windward side of the tower. With the dwindling light, he'd wanted to get as much done on that side as they could. But the light was failing.

"Good," Rose said. "My arms are killing me." She rolled her shoulders.

"Why didn't you say so?" Evan put down his roller and walked to where she stood. From behind her, he massaged her shoulders, feeling the layers of clothes she had on under her coveralls. "You don't have to do this. You can spend your evenings trying to get some sleep. I know a doctor. Maybe she can prescribe something for you."

He hoped to break through whatever mood she was in. It appeared to work. Rose's laughter was a tinkle of sound. She leaned her head back. It was the reaction Evan expected. In doing so, however, the wind blew the ponytail streaming out of her cap, and the scent of her hair made him instantly aware of her as more than a fellow painter, and brought back the feel of his hands plowing through the silky mass.

"That feels so good," she said, hanging on to the *o*. Evan heard the pleasure in her voice. He was a man who worked with words, understood their strength, knew how the nuances of delivery could touch emotions. But he'd never realized how much they could manipulate hormones. Yet, that's what Rose had done.

An Important Message from the Publisher

Dear Reader,

Because you've chosen to read one of our fine novels, I'd like to say "thank you"! And, as a special way to say thank you, I'm offering to send you two more Kimani Romance novels and two surprise gifts – absolutely FREE! These books will keep it real with true-to-life African American characters that turn up the heat and sizzle with passion.

Please enjoy the free books and gifts with our compliments...

Linda Gill

Publisher, Kimani Press

Peel off Seal and Place Inside...

FREE GIFT SEAL
PUBLISHER'S THANK YOU

THE EDITOR'S "THANK YOU" FREE GIFTS INCLUDE:

▶ Two NEW Kimani Romance™ Novels

▶ Two exciting surprise gifts

YES! I have placed my Editor's "thank you" Free Gifts seal in the space provided at right. Please send me 2 FREE books, and my 2 FREE Mystery Gifts. I understand that I am under no obligation to purchase anything further, as explained on the back of this card.

PLACE FREE GIFTS SEAL HERE

DETACH AND MAIL CARD TODAY!

168 XDL EF2N   368 XDL EF2Y

FIRST NAME

LAST NAME

ADDRESS

APT.#   CITY

STATE/PROV.   ZIP/POSTAL CODE

Thank You!

(K-ROM-11/06)

The Reader Service — Here's How It Works:

If offer card is missing write to: The Reader Service, 3010 Walden Ave., P.O. Box 1867, Buffalo, NY 14240-1867

BUSINESS REPLY MAIL

FIRST-CLASS MAIL   PERMIT NO. 717-003   BUFFALO, NY

POSTAGE WILL BE PAID BY ADDRESSEE

THE READER SERVICE
3010 WALDEN AVE
PO BOX 1867
BUFFALO NY 14240-9952

NO POSTAGE
NECESSARY
IF MAILED
IN THE
UNITED STATES

"Are you hungry?" Evan said, deflecting his body's direction with another form of pleasure.

"I'll get something at home."

"You look tired. Why don't we go to Maxwell's and then you can turn in early." He didn't give her time to refuse. He assumed her silence was agreement and started cleaning up. When they went to their cars, he opened the door for her and she got in without a word.

The dinner hour at Maxwell's Restaurant was populated with the singles in town. When Evan and Rose entered, the place wasn't crowded, but more than the expected number of patrons were seated at the various tables or in the booths lining one wall. The opposite wall contained a counter. All eyes turned to them as the bell above the door announced their entry. Smiles abounded when they were recognized. Rose walked to a booth in the middle of the wall and Cassie Maxwell came over, coffeepot in one hand, menus in the other.

"Hi Doc…Evan," she said.

Cassie Maxwell was a third-generation owner of the restaurant. Her grandmother opened it when her husband died at sea. It passed to her mother and then to Cassie.

Both Evan and Rose refused coffee and ordered the day's special—meat loaf. Evan looked around the small eatery. The walls had few adornments.

A couple of pictures hung over the booths. The floor was a checkerboard pattern of yellow-and-black tiles.

The tables were sturdy like the mast of a ship. The chairs were captain's chairs, and small replicas of the lighthouse were the candlestick holders on each table. Cassie only put them out for dinner.

"Different, isn't it?" Rose said when his attention came back to her.

"What?"

"This place." Her glance encompassed the entire restaurant. "Different from anyplace you'd eat in D.C."

"There are no places like this in D.C."

"Is that good or bad?"

"Neither. It's just different." Her words were underlined with a note of challenge, as if she wanted to debate the merits of eating in a small town. Evan could tell there was something on her mind, and he wondered what it was.

"Did you like Boston?" he asked, apparently out of the blue.

She raised her eyebrows and hunched her shoulders. "It was all right."

"But you like Lighthouse better?"

"It's my home," she hedged.

"So."

"So what?"

"So, that's not an answer. A place isn't like family. Just because you're from here doesn't mean you have to like it. Or even that you're stuck with it. You can't change family. They're yours forever, but if you don't like a place, you can leave it. So do you like Lighthouse better than Boston?"

She didn't immediately answer. She looked at him, but her mind wasn't seeing him. Then she looked past him through the front window of the restaurant to the street and town outside. Evan didn't think she saw that either.

"I have bad memories associated with Boston."

"Your marriage?"

She said nothing, only looked at her hands.

"Suppose you married someone here in Lighthouse and he died," Evan said. "Would you have bad memories of this place too? Where would you go then?"

"I don't have to listen to this." Rose moved to get up. Evan stopped her with his hand.

"Don't," he said. "I'm sorry. I didn't mean to upset you." She relaxed and sat back. "We won't talk about it."

"We seem to have a lot of subjects we don't talk about."

Evan knew exactly what she meant. He'd probed her life, but had shared little of his own.

"Rose," he began, but she raised her hand to stop him.

"You'll be returning to D.C. in a few weeks. There's no need for us to get any deeper into each other's lives."

"Any deeper than we already are." Evan finished a sentence she'd left unvoiced. "Rose, did something happen today? Did you lose a patient?"

She shook her head. "All my patients are fine."

"Then what's wrong?"

"Can we just go home?" she asked.

Neither of them had finished their meal. Evan paid the bill and they left the restaurant. They didn't say much on the short drive. He parked his SUV and got out to walk Rose to her door.

"I'll be all right from here," she said.

"I'll see you to the door." Evan deliberately didn't touch her. He pulled the small gate open and they walked toward her steps.

"Good night, Evan." Her voice was short but quick as if he'd done something wrong.

"Rose, won't you tell me what's wrong. Did I do something?"

She faced the door, her hand on the knob, her head bowed. "It's not you," she said.

"Then what happened?" Evan asked. Rose had her key out and was fitting it into the lock. She stopped when he asked the question.

For a long moment she appeared paralyzed in place. She didn't move or look up. Her key remained halfway in the lock. Without turning, she said, "Today would have been my first anniversary."

Evan stared at the closed door. Rose had melted into the darkness and disappeared while he was reeling from the gunshot blast she'd delivered.

He turned away, looking into the darkness, punctuated at regular intervals by the revolution of the constant sweep of light. He hesitated as he looked at the steps to the ground. For a moment he too was suspended by indecision. Rose obviously didn't want his company. Yet she'd looked so miserable, how could he not want to help her?

Evan turned back, looking at the imposing door as if it were the barrier to a cave. Did she really want to be alone? he wondered. Or was this a defense mechanism? He knew about those. He'd practiced them for two years, hiding what he really wanted, and thought, from all those who could have helped him. He'd become a master at it, until his mind and body rebelled. He was lucky there were people around who cared about him. Rose was cloistered inside her home—alone.

Decisively, he stepped back to the door and punched the doorbell. He could hear it ringing inside. He was certain Rose was protecting herself.

He rang the bell again. And a third time before he could see her shadowy figure approaching through the beveled glass.

"Do you really want to be alone tonight?" he asked the moment the entry door swung inward.

For a millisecond her face remained stoic. Then she crumbled and flung herself into his arms. Evan caught her, holding her tightly and backing her into the room. He kicked the door shut and heard the latch engage. He stood with his arms around her and hers around him for an eternity. She didn't resort to tears as he'd expected, but held him as if she needed the contact with another living, breathing human.

Evan's night on the Allison Avenue bridge came back to him. He'd been in the same state. Lost. Alone. Wanting desperately to escape the demons that plagued him. When the tightness of her arms relaxed, he turned her to his side and walked her into the great room.

Evan had been in Rose's house his first night back in Lighthouse. But today was the first time he really looked around. The place was different. The Early American furniture her parents preferred had been replaced with a traditional sofa and love seat. The color scheme was a soft rose with deep maroon and beige accents. The room reminded him of her.

The real her.

Not the person she showed the world, but the

one who resided inside her. Probably the one that Brett had known. They sat, still holding on to each other, on the sofa.

Rose moved her bare feet up beside her, continuing to lean on Evan. Her head was on his shoulder and her arms around his waist. He smelled her hair and that scent that defined her. A faint hint of the white paint from the lighthouse and the ocean air were also present. Yet it was her, packaged and complete, an aroma that would forever bring her to his mind.

"I'm sorry," Evan said. "I didn't know."

"Of course you didn't." She shifted to look at him. Her head remained on his shoulder. "How could you?"

"Do you want to talk about it?" Evan asked.

Rose shook her head. "It might help," Evan prompted. "Why don't you tell me about Brett."

"I've already told you."

"You told me his name, what he did, not who he was, what he thought. Tell me that."

"You really want to hear it?"

He nodded. He was unsure if he really did want to hear about her husband, but she needed to hear herself tell the story.

Rose took a deep breath. Evan felt her body expand and contract as she took in and exhaled breaths. She pushed away from him and sat up.

Evan reluctantly let her go. She pulled her hair free of the ponytail, and it flowed around her shoulders, making her face soft. He hadn't turned on any lights when they'd come into the room. The hall light shone through the archway. In the dimness her eyes had a dreamy look to them.

"Brett was a happy person. Full of life. Liked to tell jokes and laugh." She smiled as if she was remembering an amusing incident. Evan didn't ask her to recount it. He liked hearing her talk. Her voice was soft and nonthreatening. And he felt she was speaking more to herself than to him.

"We talked all the time. Made plans to do things we both knew we'd never do—go hang gliding, skiing, bungee jumping. It was fun. Brett's way of letting me know he'd get better." She looked at Evan then. Her face glowed with memory. "The planning was fun. We'd imagine what it was like, tell each other how it would feel. The wind against our faces, the surge of expectation when you jumped from a high place. These were all experiences we shared with each other."

Evan took her hand. He felt as if she was listening to her own heart. And that Brett had entered the room. He didn't interrupt her but let her continue.

"He was a wizard on the computer. He played

it like a piano. His hands moved so fast I couldn't follow them. He wrote his own programs."

Rose glanced at him and smiled. Evan smiled too. Talking seemed to have pushed away the sadness in her eyes.

"The computer was his whole world."

"Until he met you?"

The sadness returned to her eyes. Evan wondered what he'd said. Rose leaned forward. She ran her arms around his waist and put her head on his chest, resuming her former position. Evan hadn't expected it and his body was suddenly thrust into a hot fire. He held his breath, then let it out slowly. With Rose's head on his chest, she couldn't miss his accelerated heartbeat.

"Can I tell you a secret, Evan?" she whispered. "Best friend to best friend?"

Evan knew they had passed the point of being friends. Even best friends. They weren't lovers. They were somewhere in between. On a plane that had no name. They were climbing a mountain, each on opposite sides. They'd met each other at the base where the ground was wide, and circumventing the mountain took a long, long time. Part of the way up, their paths crisscrossed, taking them through a wedge of rock so narrow and steep that they had to hold on to each other in the rarefied air to survive. Once that point was crossed they went on walking together, but each having to reach the next level in order to cross the threshold at the top. While they were still on the road, unless one of them turned back, they were destined to reach that precipice at which there would be no return.

"You can always talk to me, Rose," Evan told her.

She waited. He thought she was deciding how to say what she wanted him to hear.

"I feel like I should be more upset," she said.

"More upset about what?"

"About today."

Evan pushed himself up on the sofa. Rose was pushed back. She looked up at him.

"Today would have been our anniversary. I forgot." Her eyes were huge as she stared at him. "I forgot until someone at the office reminded me."

"Rose, you were busy. You're a doctor." He gave her an easy excuse, even though he knew being busy could make her forget everything else.

"I know," she said. "And the office was packed today, but it would have been our first anniversary. How could I forget it?"

"Because Brett isn't here. He's not around for you to see every day. To be reminded of the happy times in your lives."

"Is that it?" She leaned closer to him, looking at him as if she needed to believe his words were true.

"Rose, you don't need excuses. You're human."

She hugged him. Her body was already across his. Evan breathed in the scent of her. His arms went around her. Evan never thought holding Rose could make him feel so good. But it did. Then she surprised him. Obviously she'd reached the summit ahead of him.

Her mouth covered his. Her arms went around his neck, holding him tightly as her tongue invaded his mouth. Pleasure alarms went off all over his body. The kiss was intense, ravishing, with a quality of desperation. Evan's arms hugged her as if that was the only place on the planet they would fit. She was soft and warm with curves that matched the contours of his hands. An energy filled him, as if Rose wasn't just kissing him but empowering him with a new spirit. He could feel it flowing through him like boiling blood racing through his body. His heart pounded in its effort to keep up with the lightning-fast speed it needed for the blood to complete its course.

Rose slid her mouth to his cheek, then drew it across his face as if she was mapping his features. Yet her design homed in on the target where she'd begun. Evan told himself he had to be in heaven. Nothing on earth could feel this good. Rose turned in his arms, swung her legs over him and sat on his lap.

Evan moaned at the delicious joy that went through him. His body was as hard as stone and he was nearing the breaking point. He held her still, directly over his arousal. By his nails, he hung on to sanity, knowing in a second he'd be beyond control.

With superhuman effort he pushed her back, breaking contact with her mouth and stopping the action between them. Somewhere in his mind logic reared its head. Honor, integrity, self-respect, he wasn't sure which came to him, but he knew tonight wasn't the right time to make love to Rose.

She looked at him; her eyes still had that dreamy look in them. He saw her need and wanted to match it. She leaned forward. Evan's hands on her waist restrained her.

"What's wrong?" she asked.

"Rose, you can be in no doubt that I want to make love to you." As if it had received a dash of ice water, her expression changed. A moment ago she was leaning toward him, now she tried to pull away. Evan stopped her with the same effort he'd used to keep her from kissing him. "Right now I feel like I'm going to explode and I'd like nothing better than to roll you over on the floor and make love to you until you scream my name loud enough for ships at sea to hear."

She looked down. Then back at him. Her eyes were liquid pools.

"But we both know I'm not the man you want tonight. I'm not Brett, and you would hate me tomorrow."

"Evan—"

He stopped her with the shake of his head. "If you found me in bed with you tomorrow morning, you'd never look at me the same again. And while there are changes I can live with, that is not one of them."

Rose slumped against him. He slid his hand up her back and held her like a baby.

"I'm sorry," she said.

"Shh," he whispered, patting her back. "Just rest. It's been a long day."

She shifted to the side, stretched out on the sofa. Evan kept his arms around her as she pillowed her head on his chest.

"Close your eyes and try to sleep."

She did as he told her. Evan closed his eyes and rested his head on the back of the sofa. Consciously he breathed. Slowly, normally drawing in air and letting it out, trying to get his body back under control.

He both heard and felt Rose's ragged inhalations. Eventually, her breath calmed and minutes later he heard the change and thought she'd fallen asleep. Evan didn't want to move her. He knew she prowled the house at night, that she didn't sleep well. When she spoke, it surprised him.

"I have a question for you, Evan."

"What is it?" Their voices were soft in the darkness, quiet as if speaking too loudly would disturb some unknown ghosts occupying the same space.

"Back in Washington. Did you leave...anyone... there?"

Evan thought about his life on the staff of a U.S. senator. There was little time for a social life outside of politics, but there were also few people he met who weren't part of the current establishment. He'd only been back in Lighthouse a few weeks, but Washington seemed light-years away. There had been a few women in his life since his divorce, but nothing serious.

"No one special," he answered. "The only special person in my life is right here."

Chapter 8

The rain started suddenly and within seconds had graduated to a downpour. Evan heard it slashing against the windows, sheeting against the house.

Rose slept soundlessly against him. Evan stroked her hair and kissed her temple. He didn't want to wake her, but he tightened his arm around her anyway. She needed someone. Even if she wouldn't admit it. And he didn't mind being that person.

Evan leaned back and breathed in the smell of her hair and the faint fragrance of the soap she used. The fireplace lay across from him, wood stacked inside ready for lighting. Evan wished he'd lit it tonight. Rain, Rose and a crackling fire would be a perfect combination and maybe a soothing one for Rose's jangled nerves.

Her mantel was full of photographs. By the light filtering from the hall, he recognized her parents and several of Rose at different ages: her first birthday party, dance school when she was twelve, high-school graduation, one of her skiing in Vermont. Evan had been on that trip. Rose skied better than he did. They'd spent a lot of time racing downhill and coming into the lodge with flushed faces for coffee and hot chocolate.

He scanned each photo carefully. Evan knew what he was looking for. He wanted to find one of Brett Patterson. Rose had to have one. It might be in her bedroom, but Evan thought she might have put one somewhere downstairs too and this was her favorite room.

He continued to look at the mantel and stopped near the end. There it was, nearly hidden behind one of Rose standing near the lighthouse. Evan glanced at her again. She was beautiful as she slept. He had the urge to kiss her but stopped himself. Carefully, he lowered her head to the sofa and slid out from under her. He put a throw pillow under her head and lifted her legs up. She moved into a comfortable position. Covering her with an afghan that was slung over a chair, he gave her another look and drew his hand down her face. She stirred but remained asleep.

Straightening up, he went to the mantle and lifted the frame down. The picture was a candid shot, even though the subject was looking directly at the camera. He sat in a leather chair in front of a battery of computers and accessories. He had dark hair and openly honest eyes. He had clean-shaven, boyish good looks, the kind that Evan often attributed to male models in magazines. Smiling at whomever was taking the picture, probably Rose, he looked as if he had everything in the world. Evan glanced at Rose and knew he had. Evan could see how Rose would be attracted to him.

The thought sent an unexpected pang of jealousy through him. Evan was nothing like this genius. How could he compete with a ghost, with someone who couldn't change?

Was he competing with Brett Patterson? Evan stared at the photo for a long moment, then replaced the frame in the exact position he'd found it. Rose needed someone and Evan was her friend. It was logical that he would want to help ease her pain. But did he want to replace her husband? Was that why he kept finding excuses to be with her? After telling himself he was here for only a short period and that getting involved was not on his agenda, he kept raising Rose to the top of his priority list.

Evan glanced at the sofa. He wanted to go to her but turned instead and headed for the kitchen. He was suddenly thirsty and heat was arousing his body. Doc Kidd had warned him to steer clear of Rose, but he'd ignored that warning.

He opened the refrigerator and found a carton of orange juice. It was practically the only thing in there. There were a couple of take-out containers from restaurants and several bottles of water, but few other things.

Evan found a glass and poured the juice. As he drank, he saw the closed door leading to the dining room. With a decided click, Evan set the glass on the counter and opened the door. Light cut a rectangle over the room's features.

The table had eight chairs around it. Evan switched on the light. Boxes covered one end of the room. Their lids hung open, exposing the jumbled contents inside.

Evan stepped into the room. The pocket doors leading to the hall across from the great room where Rose slept, were closed. Evan hadn't turned on a light in the kitchen but pressed the wall switch near the entrance. The chandelier shone brightly on the white tablecloth and the stack of computers at the other end of the room. This must be Brett's equipment, Evan thought. On the table were papers. He looked at them, expecting more wedding cards or their marriage license.

What he saw was a huge envelope from a medical school and one from Portland Hospital. That one had Mark Carey handwritten above the return address. Several envelopes that looked like bank statements had a Boston address. Feeling suddenly uncomfortable, he backed up to the light and switched it off. Then he closed the door and turned around.

"Rose!" Fear laced through him. His heart nearly stopped when he found her outlined in the dark. He could only say, "I'm sorry. I didn't mean to pry."

She looked away from him. The rain had stopped and the wind provided the only noise in the dark kitchen. Evan couldn't see her expression. He didn't know if she was angry with him. She had every right to be. Rose picked up his glass from the counter and drank the remainder of the juice.

Then she walked to the door and opened it. She switched on the lights, the same as he had done. "These are mainly things we had in Boston," she said in a voice as calm as if she were sleepwalking. "My parents packed up the apartment and brought everything here. I didn't know what to do with it all."

"Rose, you don't have to do this," Evan said.

"And what about all the equipment?" She turned her gaze on the computers at the opposite end of the room. "Should I donate it to a school, give it away to some deserving charity?" She stopped as soon as her voice began to rise. Keeping control of herself, she went on. "I have to do something about the banks in Boston, but the rest of it, it just seemed easier to leave it alone, close the door and…"

"Pretend it's not there?" Evan finished for her.

"Something like that. I know it doesn't make the problem disappear, but it postpones it for a while."

"Take my word for it, Rose, that is not a good idea."

She gave him a strange look. Evan knew she was thinking of his promise to tell her what had brought him back to Lighthouse. He would tell her, but not tonight. She already had enough on her mind. She didn't need to add another problem she would immediately try to solve.

The grandfather clock in the hall counted out nine o'clock when Rose closed the door on the past and the two of them returned to the great room.

"I left my drink in the kitchen," Evan said.

"I'll get it," Rose said. "I'm thirsty, too."

Evan glanced around the room. He saw the fire-place and for a moment a flash blinded them. Closing his eyes, he willed the image to go away. He was still standing in the middle of the room staring at the grate when Rose returned with a tray. She set it on the coffee table and took her seat on the sofa.

"What are we having?" Evan inhaled.

"Spiced apple cider," Rose confirmed. "And popcorn."

He sat down on the floor, his back against the sofa.

The dining room was still on his mind. He saw it for what it was—Rose's version of the office. The one that she would someday trash, as Evan had, if she didn't let out the feelings she was holding inside.

"I suppose you already knew about the boxes." Rose brought up the subject that was on his mind.

"It started with the photo." He looked up at the frame he'd pulled out from behind her picture. "I wanted to know what he looked like."

Rose followed his gaze. "I'd forgotten the photo was there. My mother took it from my bedroom after we came back here. She put it there."

"You loved him an awful lot, didn't you?" Evan held his breath for her answer. He had popcorn in one hand and his mug of cider in the other. Both hands remained stationary as he waited for her answer.

Rose put her mug on the table and stretched out on the sofa. "Yes, I did," she said in a voice Evan had never heard before. It was as soft as velvet and reverent too. "In all this time, no one has asked me that question. They offered me pity, platitudes and sometimes disguised insults. They couldn't seem to conceive that I could love someone when I knew he was ill. That I'm somehow better off because he died early in our marriage."

Her hand touched his shoulder and Evan forced himself to remain still. The unexpected contact sent an explosion of emotions through him. At the same time the logs in the fireplace shifted and a flurry of sparks and flames shot against the screen.

Evan reached up and covered her hand. "How do you feel now, Rose? Are you still in love with him? Can you pick up your life and go on?"

Slowly she slipped her hand from his embrace. "I don't know," she said.

The ringing phone jarred Rose awake. As a resident at Mass General she'd learned to open her eyes and be instantly awake. All the residents used to compare their duty training to that of the Navy Seals, sleeping in fifteen-minute intervals and always ready for combat.

She woke, moving and reaching at the same time. Forgetting she wasn't in her bed, she fell off the sofa. Something broke her fall. Looking up, she saw Evan. Memory raced into her brain like fire up an air vent. The two of them stared at each other for the space of one ring.

Rose scrambled to her feet and snatched up the phone. She already knew it was an emergency. The phone only rang at night when there was one.

"Dr. Albright," she spoke as calmly as she could with thoughts of Evan taking precedence over most of her consciousness.

"Emergency, Doctor." She recognized Carl Andersson's voice. He was the police chief. "Jim Wiley fell off the roof of his house."

"Where is he?" Rose didn't bother asking questions like how it happened.

"At his house, 39 Maple Road. Paramedics on-site."

"What about Medevac?"

"They're waiting for you to make the call. But he's got two broken arms, both legs and bleeding from the head."

"Call them. I'm on my way."

Rose hung up and headed for the door. She grabbed her jacket from the coat tree. Her medical bag was in the Jeep. The ambulance on-site would be fully equipped with anything else she might need.

"Rose?"

She turned, surprised to find Evan in the archway. She had forgotten he was there. "I have to go, Evan."

"What happened?"

"Student fell from a roof." She walked fast. With what the police chief had said on the phone, she didn't expect Jim would live until she got there.

"Who?" Evan asked, keeping time with her movement.

"Jim Wiley."

"He's one of my students. I'm going with you."

Rose didn't want him to go. He'd be a distraction, but she had no time to argue with him. Jim was probably critical and seconds counted. Moments later she was speeding through town. The Jeep was equipped with a siren light on the dash. She also had a portable one that she'd placed on the roof, and she switched them on. The red light whirled around, but she didn't turn on the sound. At this hour the streets in Lighthouse were deserted and there was no need to wake up babies with the noise.

Evan sat quietly staring directly in front of him. Rose took a moment to check his posture. He was tense. His hands were on his knees, but not in a relaxed manner, more like a hunting dog on point.

As she turned on to Maple Road the street was

lit up as if Christmas had come early. The fire department truck blocked any cars that might want to go north or south on the residential street. One of the town's two ambulances sat in front of 39 Maple flanked by two police cars. Multiple red-and-blue lights revolved in blinding intensity, throwing garish illumination on the neighbors who'd come out to see what was going on. Rose was out of the Jeep the moment she threw the gearshift into Park.

Naturally she looked up at the roof on her way inside the yellow police tape that had cordoned off the area. Maple Road was in the old part of the town. It was where the wealthy had always lived. The homes were big and stately, with steeply slanted roofs. She couldn't imagine what Jim was doing up on the roof in the middle of the night. She checked her watch out of habit. It was nearly midnight.

"We've stopped the bleeding and immobilized him," one of the paramedics said. "Blood pressure is low. Four broken bones."

Rose saw they had taped his legs together and secured his arms. "I called for Medevac." She knelt down and examined Jim. His face was contorted in pain, but he was alive. An IV had been inserted in his hand. "Jim, it's Dr. Rose."

He focused on her for a second. Then his eyes rolled back in his head. She looked into his eyes with her light, examined him as much as she could and checked his pressure again.

"He's bleeding internally," she said to the paramedics. "We need to get him out of here as soon as possible. Seconds count."

She looked at Jim's face. His eyes were closed. "I want you to stay awake," she said calmly. "It's important. We're taking you to Portland. Promise me you'll stay awake?"

"Mom," he said in a raspy whisper. Rose looked around for the Wileys and saw Evan standing next to them. Rose thought he had his eyes closed. Her gaze swung from him to the Wileys. Someone had grabbed a couple of the blankets from the fire truck and Mr. Wiley had wrapped one around himself and his wife. She'd stopped crying, although she moved back to her husband and clutched his arm tight. Rose motioned for them to come closer.

"Do you know your name?" Rose asked Jim. She needed to see if he was coherent. His chances of survival increased dramatically if he knew what was happening. Jim didn't answer her, but called again for his mother.

"They're coming. You need to go to the hospital in Portland." As if on cue, she heard the blades of the helicopter. It would land on the high-school football field. Lighthouse was a place with many hills and trees. The football field was both flat and unobstructed enough for it to land.

As the Wileys reached the side of their son, Rose had her hands on his abdomen. "Jim," she called. "Stay with me. No sleeping. You can sleep later. Tonight I need you awake."

"I'm so tired."

"I know you are, but you have to stay awake."

She looked up at the Wileys. "Is he going to be all right?" Mrs. Wiley asked. Tears were in her voice.

Rose looked at one of the paramedics and nodded. She moved aside, keeping the Wileys out of the way while the two men lifted the board they'd slipped under Jim and put it on a gurney. Evan stood several feet away. He had his arm around Katrina Wiley, Jim's twelve-year-old sister. She looked frightened, clutching her kitten close to her chest. Rose smiled at the little girl, hoping to make her feel that things would be all right. She couldn't tell her that. If Jim was lucky he'd get to Portland in time.

The paramedics started to roll him away. Mrs. Wiley stepped forward to go with them. Rose blocked her.

"Just a moment," she said. When Jim was out of sight, she said, "I know you want to go with him and you will. They won't leave without you."

"Doctor," Mr. Wiley said, clutching his blanket around his arms.

"He's critical," Rose said. Mrs. Wiley's knees gave, but her husband held her up. "We'll alert the hospital to be ready for him." She looked at Mrs. Wiley. Putting her arm around her, Rose whispered, "Hold it together. He's going to need you." Mrs. Wiley sniffed and fought back the tears. "Now, go. The helicopter is waiting."

"Katrina?" her father said.

"We'll take care of her until you come back." Rose looked at the woman who spoke. Helen Talbott lived next door to the Wileys. She ran a nursery school and was dressed in a nightgown covered by a raincoat. Helen opened her arms and Katrina left Evan's side and ran into them. Rose heard her crying.

The Wileys headed for the ambulance. Rose followed. "Follow me to the high school," she ordered Evan. Rose took in his appearance. He looked grey under the flashing lights. There was something wrong. She saw sweat on his forehead as she passed him. She had no time to stop and see if he needed anything. Jim's condition commanded she give him priority. She touched Evan's arm, held it for a moment as her eyes met his vacant ones. "Meet me at the high school," she said again, hoping to reach him. Then she jumped into the ambulance and it sped away.

Rose looked at Evan through the small window in the back. He stood where she'd left him. People moved away, returning to their homes. The drivers of the fire trucks and police cars moved toward their vehicles. In moments the place would be deserted. Yet Evan stood as if rooted to the street.

Lighthouse, Maine, wasn't the kind of place with twenty-four-hour anything. The cliché of rolling up the sidewalks after dark applied to the small town. Unless there was a night football game or school dance, the town was effectively closed for the evening.

So it should have been easy to find one solitary figure walking the streets. But Evan had eluded her with his hiding place. He hadn't followed her to the helicopter. Her Jeep was exactly where she'd left it on Maple Road when the paramedics dropped her off.

The lighthouse was her first choice after checking that he wasn't at home. His SUV sat in the driveway empty of his physical presence yet complete with his essence. Even in the cold, she could feel him there.

Driving through town, she wondered where he could be. She knew something was wrong. Something had happened tonight on Maple Road. Then it occurred to her. Turning the Jeep in a tight

U-turn, she headed for the Allison Avenue bridge. Her headlights illuminated him standing in the same position where she'd seen him that first night, when he'd returned to Lighthouse. She turned the lights off and let the Jeep roll to a stop.

He didn't look at her when she headed for him. Her shoes make no sound on the concrete, but in the quiet of the night, he had to know he was no longer alone.

She stopped three feet from where he stood. "You had a panic attack." It was a statement.

Evan looked down at the water then up at the dark horizon. "Yes," he said, not elaborating. "How did you know?"

"You looked as gray as a ghost. When I passed you on my way to the ambulance, you were sweating even though the wind was blowing. You held your teeth together to keep them from chattering, and even though your body was present, your mind was somewhere else. Where were you?"

"I was on Maple Road."

He wasn't helping her, but Rose wasn't deterred. She knew he was holding things inside. It was the way he'd survived, and letting go wasn't something he was used to doing. "How long have you been having these attacks?"

Evan straightened. Rose watched his hand go

into his pocket. She didn't see what he had in it, but moonlight glinted off something metal before it disappeared.

"Since I've been here? Three times."

"Are you ready to tell me what's causing them? What happened tonight to bring this one on?"

"Dr. Albright, I'm sure you know that there are no reasons for panic attacks. They just happen and often even the victim doesn't know why."

He spoke sharply to her. Rose wanted to shout back that she was just trying to help, trying to understand, but she took a mental step back and remembered she was a doctor. Evan wasn't speaking to her, his friend, his almost lover. He was rebelling against her authority, her knowledge, her years of schooling that should have made her find the answer to help him, but he knew she was as much in the dark as he was.

Rose took a step toward him. He leaned on the railing and listened to the rushing water below. Tonight there was a moon and they could see the reflection off the surface. She stood next to him, her arms resting along the railing the same as his. Only a sliver of space separated them. She felt him trembling the same as he had the first night.

For a long moment they looked at the darkness, neither speaking. Then Rose reached over and took his hand. She pulled it toward her. Stepping closer, she wrapped it around her, hoping to recapture the closeness they'd had at her house when two best friends held each other.

"Best friends?" she asked.

"How do you do it?" Evan said. There was reverence in his voice as if the two of them stood in a church, the bridge over them representing the high arching gables of their sanctuary. "With all the demons in your own life, how do you handle emergencies so calmly? Then put yourself aside and come searching for me and take my fears away."

Rose felt as if the spirits had all settled around her, wishing her well and warming her in their protective hands.

"Emergencies like Jim Wiley don't happen every day."

"How is Jim?" he asked.

"It's too early to tell, but it doesn't look good. If he survived until he got to Portland… I'll find something out later tonight."

"You worry about everyone in this town, don't you?"

She nodded. A lump formed in her throat and she couldn't speak over it.

"What about me?"

She faced him. "You, I care about deeply. I want you to trust me…." She stopped him when he started to speak. "I want you to talk to me. When you return to Washington, I want you to go back whole, without the demons that led you to this bridge."

"That's why you touched me before you got in the ambulance."

"I was trying to reach you. Pull you back from wherever you'd gone, from whatever the trauma was that was claiming you. But I had to consider Jim first."

"I'll tell you all about it, Rose. But not tonight. You had a long day and an even longer night. You need to recharge your batteries."

"Do I have your promise on that? You will tell me?"

Evan raised his right hand. "I do solemnly promise that I will faithfully execute the office of Best Friend of Rosamund Albright, and will to the best of my ability—"

"Stop it," she interrupted his spoof of the president's oath of office.

"If you won't tell me now, at least let me see what's in your pocket."

"Why?"

"It's one of the things you do when you're in this state. I noticed it the first night you came back. After we had dinner at my house, you kept putting your hand in your pocket."

She waited. Time extended so long, she didn't think he was going to comply with her request. But his hand went in his pocket and he laid a small silver rattle in her palm.

"It was Gabe's. He was my son."

Evan slipped his arms around her waist and that's how they stood, embracing, until the sun broke over the horizon.

Chapter 9

The For Sale sign that had been forced into the hard ground in front of Doc Kidd's house last summer lay against the wall of his clapboard-style home. Rose eyed it as she knocked on the door later that morning. Doc's doorbell hadn't worked since the Carter administration. He'd never fixed it because he said he liked the quiet. When door-to-door salespeople or political campaigners rang the bell, he could silently ignore them. But come Halloween, the door was always open.

"Rose!" He stepped back and offered her entry. "Come on in." Doc Kidd's hair was thin and totally white. His face was blistered with spots, freckles, moles and skin conditions associated with age. They matched the ones on his arms and hands. His eyes had lost that piercingly blue color Rose remembered from her childhood, but they still reflected the trust that all doctors should collect along with their medical school degrees.

Boxes sat everywhere. "Packing up so soon?" she asked. Doc wasn't due to leave for Arizona until January.

"I thought I'd get a jump on things. This is stuff I won't need for the next few months. It takes me longer to do things these days, so I don't want to wait for the last minute."

"Good idea," Rose agreed. She was going to miss Doc. He'd taken her under his wing a year ago and had been available for consultations whenever she needed one.

"I was taking a breather," he said. "Made myself some tea. Wanna join me?"

She nodded and moments later they were seated in his sunny kitchen with steaming cups of tea in front of them.

"Have you sold the house?" she asked. "I see the sign is no longer on the lawn."

"Family from over in Seaverton is taking the house. Says they want to be closer to his job at the plant. Husband, wife and two kids. It'll be good to have children here again."

Rose had thought Doc Kidd should have been a pediatrician. He loved children, always had toys and treats for them.

"I wish it was another doctor."

"Lighthouse could use another one for sure. Sorry I never acted on building that clinic."

"You shouldn't have to do that, Doc. That's something the town should take up." Rose knew the present committee would do nothing. Even with Doc on the committee, the council dragged its feet, delayed proceedings and funding. If they could call a meeting on the color of the lighthouse, their ideas of what the town needed really were too low. She made up her mind not to vote for them in the next election.

"What brings you out here this morning?" Doc sat back in his chair and directed his stare at her.

"Post-traumatic stress disorder."

"PTSD?" His brows went up. "Evan Harper?"

The mug stopped halfway to Rose's mouth. "How did you know?"

"If it was anyone else, you'd have been here already." He smiled at her and sipped his tea. "And I observed him at the Final Day sail."

"I've never seen PTSD, but I think that's what it is."

"Have you asked him?"

"He's quieter than a secret agent." She paused. "I've asked him to tell me what is wrong. He won't. Until he had a panic attack the night Jim Wiley fell off the roof, I hadn't thought of it."

"How is Jim?"

"It's still too early to tell. He's been downgraded from critical to very serious and he's responding to treatment. The doctors are cautious. Looking ahead, they say he'll have a long recovery. But he's one lucky young man. That fall should have killed him." Rose relived the emotions that had gone through her when she saw his broken body lying on the ground. Thankfully, the tree in front of his house broke his fall. She shivered inwardly, her heart pumping and her teeth clenched together as she had worked to save his life.

"Did you find out what he was doing on the roof at midnight?"

"Trying to retrieve his sister's kitten."

"Katrina loves that animal."

"Yeah, she only leaves it to go to school. Anyway, with the downgrade to his condition I'm hoping he'll make a full recovery."

"He's a strong boy. A lot of fight in him. He's getting the best care possible." Doc was always optimistic.

Rose had once been that way too, but she'd had her own fall.

"Back to Evan," Doc Kidd said. "Tell me what you know."

Rose outlined his symptoms. "Sleeplessness, bad dreams, panic attacks, nervousness."

"Is he on any medication?"

"He says no."

"Have you spoken to his doctor in D.C.?"

She shook her head. "I know he has one. He's made references to a psychotherapist, but he hasn't formally or informally asked me for medical advice. In fact, he's refused it."

"So you don't know what could cause his attacks or what trauma he endured?"

She shook her head. "Inside me there's a conflict between being his concerned friend and his right to privacy."

"But if you believe medically he needs treatment, then you have every right to breach those rights."

"Only if I think there's a threat to his person or someone else. I'm sure there isn't."

"So why are you here?"

Rose looked into her cup. She didn't want anything to show on her face. She was in love with Evan Harper. She knew now that she probably always had been.

"There's no use hiding it, Rose. I've known how you felt about Evan since you two were in school."

Rose stared at Doc Kidd but didn't deny her feelings. "You worked at Walter Reed Army Hospital once. You must have seen people with PTSD."

"I did." He nodded. His expression changed and Rose could tell he was seeing the faces of former soldiers.

"What should I look for?"

"There are three main symptom types. The victim reexperiences the event, becomes emotionally numb or has increased awareness to things. He may have flashbacks, recurrences of the event while awake, nightmares or difficulty sleeping, irritability, angry outbursts, exaggerated responses or emotional and physical reactions to someone or something that reminds him of the trauma. Then he can withdraw or detach himself from others."

Rose had seen a lot of those traits in Evan. From the night she found him on the bridge she knew there was something bothering him. Until last night, when she saw his face covered in sweat did everything suddenly fall in place.

"The usual treatment for PTSD is psychotherapy." Doc Kidd's voice interrupted her thoughts. He put his mug down and leaned forward. "If Evan is reliving the event, that can trigger a panic attack. If you've been trying to get him to talk, keep at it, but don't confront him. He'll tell you in his own time."

Evan had promised Rose that he would tell her the reason for his panic attacks. He'd given her no time frame for the confession, only his word that it would happen. She latched on to that.

In the years she'd known him, he'd never broken a promise.

The sound of an automobile had Evan's heart pumping faster. He checked his watch. Rose was early. Life between them had changed after their night on the bridge. They knew the danger of getting closer, so they'd retreated to the familiar parameters of their former friendship. Evan knew it was best for the two of them. He pushed his wishes for something more to the back of his mind, knowing they shouldn't take any further steps that would move them closer to heartache. His time in Lighthouse was drawing to an end.

"Evan." Someone, not Rose, called his name. Evan turned toward the sound. Jeff Altman stood on the ground below. He'd pushed his hat back, angled his head up and balanced his hands on his hips.

"Yeah," Evan said. He frowned when he recognized Jeff. He didn't want another fight with the town councilman.

"What are you doing?" Jeff shouted.

"Come on up," Evan called down to him. He wasn't about to have a conversation from twenty feet up in the air. In the last week he and Rose had made headway on the structure. They were two-thirds the way up. In another week the entire thirty-four feet would be white and gleaming. The cap over the light room would shine black in the bright sunlight. And the lenses inside would continue to reflect the light out to sea and onto the town.

Jeff was huffing and out of breath by the time he climbed through the graduated ladders to reach Evan's position.

"Jeff, what can I do for you?" Evan asked, not waiting for the older man to gain his breath.

"What are you doing?"

Evan wanted to ask him if that was a trick question, but Jeff looked too tired to engage in friendly banter. "I'm painting the lighthouse."

"Yes, but you're using white paint."

"I can see why you got on the council, Jeff. Nothing gets by you." He couldn't resist the dig.

"This is not the color we decided on."

"Technically, it is," Evan said.

"I don't understand."

Evan continued painting. He looked over his shoulder at Jeff. "Wanna help? I got an extra roller."

Jeff sputtered and looked down at his clothes. He was wearing a suit with a light blue shirt and striped tie. Over this he wore what Evan called his councilman's coat. He must have a closet full of them, since he wore it all the time.

"Not today," Jeff said.

"I should be finished in another week."

"I see that you're making great progress, but could we get back to the color?" Jeff was a nervous man, easily flustered, and despite his personal opinion of himself, he should never have been elected to the council. He didn't have the foresight to determine what was best for the town.

"What about the color?" Evan was being intentionally obtuse.

"The vote at the town meeting was for a red-and-white color scheme. You're painting it totally white."

"Jeff, we voted on a design, not a paint color."

"What?" Jeff's face turned red in the wind and his frustration in trying to deal with Evan who was being intentionally dense.

"I put the design in. And I painted it."

"Where is the other color?"

"Didn't need another color. Decided both the diamonds and swirls would be white."

Jeff looked down at the lower part of the tower. "I don't see any difference."

"There isn't one," Evan said seriously. "I realized the town didn't really want anything but white. So I'm obliging them."

"Why, then, did we need that meeting?"

"We didn't, but then I didn't call it." Evan went back to rolling paint over the surface.

"I swear, I will never understand you."

"Jeff, if anyone asks, just tell them the design is the same but I ran out of paint and had to use the only color available."

The wind grabbed at Jeff's hat and pulled it off. He whirled around and grabbed it with an agility Evan didn't think he possessed.

As Jeff fought to keep his hat, Rose reached the top of the scaffolding and approached them. "Hello, Jeff. What are you doing here?"

Jeff glanced at Evan. "Trying to get a straight answer out of someone...*from away.*"

He walked past Rose and started his descent. Rose looked up at Evan. "What did you tell him?" Being from away was usually attributed to anyone not from Maine. The way Jeff had said it, it was an insult, especially when directed at someone who was born and reared only a few yards from the tower he was painting.

"Why the lighthouse is white."

* * *

A good night's sleep. Evan never thought he'd get one again, but since he'd watched the sun rise on the Allison Avenue bridge with Rose in his arms, he'd slept soundly. Dreamlessly. Restfully. He enjoyed it, almost as much as he enjoyed having Rose within reach. He wanted her here, in his bed, close to him. He wanted her naked, her body stretched out along the length of his. Then he remembered the calendar and nixed that idea. In less than a month he'd be packing up to leave. Returning to his life.

To the real world.

He wouldn't leave Rose with a broken heart, not after what she'd been through, and he didn't want to carry one back with him. He'd come here to mend his wounded psyche, not to create an even greater mess and leave it behind.

Their last week of painting had been companionable, but he felt there was more going on with Rose under the surface. He knew it was with himself. He'd find himself looking at her when her back was turned, remembering her weight as she slept on him and the sheer joy that went through him when he held her.

He should have called her when he finished painting the roof of the lamp house. The job was completed exactly as he'd told Jeff it would be. A week after the councilman left, frustrated and confused, the entire job was finished. Yet instead of calling Rose, he'd spent the evening alone. He'd gone for a long run and finished it with a soak in the oversize bathtub his parents had installed in the master bathroom. The kinks in his muscles eased and relaxed. Then he climbed into bed early, opening his history textbook with the intention of reading the next section, but he'd fallen into a contented and dreamless sleep. When he woke, the sun was high in the sky. Rose was the first person to come to mind. The previous night's resolve evaporated with the sunshine. He wanted to see her.

Evan's stomach growled. Maybe he'd invite Rose to breakfast. He looked at the clock. Make that lunch, he thought.

Although it was Saturday and she had office hours, she had to eat too. He hadn't been to her office, but there was only one medical building in town. Doc Kidd's office was there. It was logical that Rose's was also in the building on Main Street.

Evan found the place with no trouble. It was where his parents had taken him to see Doc Kidd whenever he was ill. Long before HMOs entered the language, Lighthouse had its own. The Medical Arts Building housed every medical service in town: Doc Kidd's office, two dentists' office and a radiology office. Anyone needing an MRI had to go to Portland.

Evan bounded up the stairs and walked through the door that had her name etched into the clear glass.

"May I—" Brenda Harrison didn't finish her question. "Evan…Evan Harper." A smile as wide as she was split her face. "It's so good to see you again. Let me have a hug." The retired high-school nurse came from behind the counter, her arms already raised. She was nearly as tall as Evan and probably outweighed him by fifty pounds. Her salt-and-pepper hair was completely white now, but her smile was as ever.

"I heard you were back in town."

"Just for a while. I'm checking out the old place."

"And teaching at the high school, I hear."

"That's Rose's fault," he said with a smile. "She roped me into it practically before I could get my feet on the ground."

"Just listen to that accent. You been away too long. You talk like someone from away." She released him.

"I've been accused of that," he said, remembering Jeff's parting words.

"And look, you're blushing." She returned to her post.

Evan felt the heat in his face. "What are you doing here? I thought after you retired you sailed off to see the world, turning in those wall posters for reality." In the nurse's office at the high school, Mrs. Harrison had had huge posters of European capitals. She said it was her dream to visit them someday.

"I tried it. After a while I just wanted to come home. Then that got a little too much for me too. Retirement wasn't something I could cope with. Too boring. So I help Rose out on weekends and when she needs me." Evan looked around the waiting room. There were several people there but none he knew. He nodded at their smiles. Brenda Harrison had been a dynamo when they were students. Always on the go. It was no surprise to Evan that she needed to be active in her retirement.

"Is Rose available around noon?"

"She finishes up early on Saturdays. I'd say another hour and she'll be free. Do you need an appointment?"

"It's not medical. I thought I'd ask her to lunch."

A smile covered Brenda's dinner-plate-size face. "That's fine. I hear you two have danced the third dance."

"What?" Evan knew this was a parable. Mainers had many parables they loved to invoke to explain any situation, but Evan wasn't familiar with this one.

"It's an old-timers' saying," Brenda explained. "At a dance, if a man dances more than twice with the same girl, the family expected a marriage proposal would be forthcoming."

"And how long ago was this third *dance* the rage?"

"Sixteenth century."

Evan squelched a laugh. "A little out of date I'd say."

"I don't know," Brenda said, raising her chin and her eyebrows as she looked at him. "You're here for lunch. Sounds like dancing to me."

Rose came out then and dropped a folder on Brenda's desk. "Evan," she said. Her face lit up with a smile. "What are you doing here?"

"He wants to take you to lunch." Brenda spoke before Evan had the chance. "I told him you'd be free in an hour."

Since neither he nor Rose had been able to speak, they looked at each other. She nodded.

"I'll be back in an hour," he said. "Good seeing you, Mrs. Harrison."

Evan waved and went out the door and down the stairs. There was an elevator wide enough for wheelchairs and gurneys, but it was slow and he preferred the steps. Maxwell's was down the street. He could wait there. The noonday crowd would be thick and Evan wondered how many of them would be thinking he was waltzing Rose around the floor for the third time?

Outside, he climbed into his SUV when an idea hit him. Checking his watch, he had just enough time to complete his plan.

"Where are we going?" Rose asked an hour later when Evan turned away from the center of town and headed up the hill that led to the lighthouse. Now that the painting wa done, the scaffolding would be removed as soon as Mr. Wanger sent a crew over to dismantle it. "We can't eat out here. It's too cold, too windy."

"There is no wind where we're going." Evan stopped next to the building, the same place he'd parked each day when he came to paint. He'd spent the last hour ordering food from the local restaurant and setting up the lighthouse. When he returned for Rose, she'd removed her lab coat and pulled her hair down. Brenda was gone and the waiting room was free of anyone needing medical services.

"Then where are we going?" she asked.

"Come on." He grabbed a shopping bag from the back of the SUV and clicked the button to close the door. Going around to Rose's side, he helped her out.

Keeping her hand in his, he led her into the building. She stopped just inside. Turning completely around, she looked at the walls. Then she looked up, putting her hand on her head as if she were wearing a hat that would fall off. She leaned back and stared all the way to the top.

A huge smile was on her face. Then she giggled. The giggle turned into a full belly laugh. Finally she sobered. "When did you do this?"

"I've been working on it all along. I did the bulk of it last week. Do you like it?"

She walked closer to one wall. Then she turned back. Her face was bright with an appreciative smile. "It's wonderful. Surprising. Unexpected."

On the inside of the lighthouse Evan had painted the approved design, the one voted on at the town meeting, the colors they had chosen. He'd kept the door closed when Rose was with him. At night he'd open it to let the paint dry. The faint smell of fresh paint still permeated the air.

"Come on, you haven't seen the best part." Evan reached for her hand and led her to the narrow winding staircase that led to the light at the top. Rose stepped onto the top platform and looked at the panorama of land and sea through the windows. It was impossible not to take in the airiness, the feeling of being suspended above the world when they stood on the same level as the lens that guided ships to safety.

She walked along the platform. Evan followed

her until she came to the area where he'd set up their lunch. Her eyes opened wider and she glanced from him to the small round table with a red-and-white-checkered tablecloth, candles and place settings for two. Evan had the food in the bag he carried.

"When did you do this?"

"I had a whole hour. Do you think it's too much?"

She grinned at him and his insides turned over. "I could do lunch like this every day." Reaching up, she kissed him quickly on the mouth. He felt it to his toes.

The chairs were set close together so they could take in the view while they ate. Together they removed the food from the bag and sat down.

"I couldn't have chosen a better place to have lunch," Rose said. "And the food is delicious."

"No waiters to interrupt us, no crowded restaurant, no view of the parking lot."

"I'll take this view any day." Rose panned the windows looking out to sea. It was a perfect day, sunny, clear sky, blue water. He could even see a ship in the distance.

"You really like it here," Evan stated.

"I love it," she confirmed. "I think it's the most beautiful place I've ever seen."

Evan didn't look at her. She was rooted to Lighthouse. There were other places to see. People lived all over the world, but Rose only wanted to be in this place.

"I used to hide out up here when I was young." Evan got up and walked to the window.

"I know," Rose said. "This was the first place I looked for you the other night. The door was locked and I couldn't get in."

He smiled. "I was keeping you out until I could show you the finished product. After we'd finish for the day, I'd come back and work in here. Then I'd open the door. Before going to work in the morning, I'd lock it. That night I didn't get the chance." He looked around, remembering the hours he'd spent here. "This was a place to get away from my parents when we were having...differences."

"I remember the night of the big storm when no one could find you," Rose said. "We were frantic that something had happened."

He laughed and took a drink of the sparkling cider he'd brought for their meal. Turning back, he looked at Rose. She remained at the table, her body turned toward him, her legs crossed. He remembered her long and shapely body in a bathing suit. She was beautiful, more so with the sun shining on her. "I thought my father was going to kill me."

"What saved you?"

"I threw his words back at him."

"What words?"

"He'd told me that if I was ever caught somewhere when it was safer to stay put than head out into danger, I should stay where I was. Of course, he was talking about drinking and driving, but I skipped that little tidbit at the time."

"That night the storm roared." He knew Rose remembered it too. People in Lighthouse still talked about it in terms of where they were at the time.

"I was too scared to try to come out. It was dark and I couldn't see anything in the lashing rain. My house was a few yards away and I couldn't see it. I feared the wind would blow me over the cliffs and I'd drown, so I stayed where I was. You know how long storms can last up here. I thought I'd starve before it ended. I'd taken nothing with me when I left the house, except attitude. When my father found me, I could tell he was seeing blood."

"He was scared for you."

"Yes." The word was simple but held a ton of meaning. His father loved him. Beyond reason. Evan understood that more now than he had at the time. After Gabe had come into and gone out of Evan's life, he understand a world of things he'd never truly known. It was like that small infant not only made him a father, but taught him the meaning of unconditional love. The kind of love that had led Evan's father to battle the winds of a northeaster to find him. And the kind that had his parents standing by his side, intuitively seeing to his needs after Gabe died.

Evan thought he knew what love meant when he was fifteen, sitting on the floor only a few feet from where he was now. He looked at the spot, recalling the whipping wind raising the ocean and throwing it against the rocks and walls of the lighthouse. It was like a being inside a hurricane. Evan had prayed his father would find him. The love he had for his parents would surely lead them to him. His father knew him, knew his heart, knew that he was afraid of what might happen.

But Evan didn't. He didn't understand fear.

It was only after Gabe that Evan learned the true meaning of love. And along with that lesson, was the equal knowledge of what it meant to be truly afraid.

Watching Evan was becoming a habit with Rose. There were times she looked for clues that something might be wrong. Other times she saw only the man he was today. This was one of those times. He stood before the panorama of windows. Rose sat at the table he'd brought up the winding steps so they could have a meal. A rush of emotion went through her.

Evan turned to face her and she began clearing the aftermath of their lunch.

"You don't have to do that," he said.

"Sure I do. You cooked, I clean." She got up and cleared all the food away. She saved the bottle of sparkling cider, refilling her glass.

"I thought about buying a bottle of wine but wouldn't want to ply the doctor with alcohol."

She laughed. "I'm off duty."

"I haven't had a drink in a long while. I did have some beers a couple of weeks ago. When I was working for the senator, there was no time for drinks unless I was at one of the parties."

"One of the glamorous parties Washington is famous for?"

Evan laughed. "Some of them are interesting. Some are work. Some are just plain fun. You'd like them."

"I don't think so. I like it here."

"It's a nice place to hide," Evan said.

"Which one of us is hiding?" she asked.

"Probably both of us, but we're not going to analyze you today."

"Are we going to analyze you?" She was afraid to ask the question. It often brought out his defense mechanisms and forced him to withdraw into himself.

"Remember that first day we came to the lighthouse, right after you found me on the Allison Avenue bridge?"

She nodded.

"You said when someone dies, you go on."

"You never forget, but you learn to live with the pain." She repeated the words she'd said that day. "Day by day it lessens. After a while you're ready to love again."

Evan hesitated for a long moment. "I lost both my wife and my son in a fire."

"Oh my God!" Rose moved then, leaving her seat and coming to stand next to him. "I am so sorry. I didn't know."

Evan didn't want her to touch him. He leaned against the windows and waited a moment. The scene came back to him as clear as if it were happening.

"Evan, don't relive it. It triggers the panic attacks."

He glanced at her, holding her gaze for a long moment.

"I know something traumatic happened. I know you're suffering from PTSD, Post trau—"

"I know what it stands for." His voice was sharp. Then he sighed. "I'm sorry."

"Then you admit you have it?"

He sat down on the floor and pulled his knees up. Resting his arms on them, he dangled the wineglass between his legs. Rose dropped down next to him. His face had begun to sweat. She took his hand and removed the glass.

He nodded finally. "It's what the doctor explained to me in D.C. I thought I had everything under control. I felt as if I was getting better. I'd begun to sleep through the night. The nightmares were gone and my sessions were positive."

"You've been having sessions while you've been here?"

"Once a week."

Rose knew she looked perplexed. "And all the while I thought you were avoiding me."

"How could anyone avoid you? You're still the same bossy girl I grew up with."

They had no past, Rose thought. She was sorry about that. She feared they had no future either and that would leave her with nothing.

"Don't get off topic," she said, protecting herself from her own thoughts.

"My ex-wife's name was Alana. We had a son, Gabriel. Called him Gabe." He stopped.

Rose pressed his hand. "Slow and steady. Don't relive it. Focus on something else. Your hands, the stairs, me. But don't live it again."

"We knew almost immediately that our marriage wasn't going to work, but we tried to hold it together. For two years we tried, but I was always at work. She felt neglected and rightly so.

We filed for divorce on a friendly basis. She found out she was pregnant after we were in divorce proceedings. We went ahead with the divorce. She didn't want custody."

Evan glanced at Rose. "Don't think ill of her."

Rose kept her expression unreadable. He obviously wanted to make sure she knew that Alana was a good person.

"When we married we didn't talk about children. We didn't talk about a lot of important things couples should before they get married. I didn't know she didn't want children. She didn't know I did. When Gabe was born I became the custodial parent. But my hours were sporadic. I had a sitter and sometimes Alana backed me up when the sitter was unavailable."

"Did she become attached to Gabe during those times?"

Evan smiled. "I think she did. She never refused me when I asked her and often had Gabe. She'd buy him presents, and when I came to pick him up she was reluctant to let him go."

Evan squeezed his hands together. A long moment passed before he spoke again. "That night I was late."

He laughed and toyed with his empty wineglass.

"Would you like more?" Rose asked.

He shook his head but kept the glass between his fingers. Rose recognized the gesture. He was keeping from transferring the past to the present. Holding on to the glass helped him remain in the lighthouse, in the moment, not back in D.C. reliving the tragedy.

"Alana took Gabe for the day. I had to work and she was free. I was late coming back. When I turned my car on to her street the place was…"

Rose waited. She watched him swallow. She said nothing, only got up and took the bottle of cider off the table. She poured it into his glass.

"The street was filled with police cars, fire engines. I could smell…could smell the smoke from blocks away. I don't remember stopping the car. Suddenly I was running, shouting for Gabe and Alana. Hands grabbed me. I pushed them off. I got past the cops, Alana's neighbors, several firefighters, before I was tackled to the ground." He shuddered with the memory. "It was too late."

Chapter 10

The air in the lighthouse was heavy. Rose rubbed her hand over Evan's shoulder and neck.

"There was nothing you could have done."

"I know. I was late getting there. If I'd been on time—"

"Stop!" she commanded. "Evan, this was not your fault."

He stared at her for almost a minute. Then nodded.

"How did the fire start?" Rose asked.

"The report said there was a gas leak. It was so senseless. I finished the speech corrections I'd been working on and took my time leaving. If I'd—"

"If you'd been on time all three of you could have died."

He looked at her. "For a while I thought that would have been better."

"I understand your pain, Evan." She really did. She'd lost someone she loved too. "How long ago did Gabe and Alana die?"

"Two years." He set the glass aside again. "I thought I'd dealt with it. I'd gotten over the pain of everyday living. After two years you'd think anyone would have completely grieved."

"Not everyone." Rose continued to run her hand along Evan's shoulder, only now instead of it being an act of comfort, it was a caress. "We all grieve differently."

"But we don't trash our offices." When Rose didn't say anything, he explained. "It was a perfectly beautiful day. Nothing was bothering me, I thought. I went into the office, turned on my computer and opened my e-mail. The next thing I remember, several guys were holding me down and my office was a shambles."

"What happened just before that?"

"Nothing," he answered quickly. "I have gone over and over that morning in my mind and nothing happened. I didn't read any of the e-mail.

I turned on the computer, but it hadn't finished booting up."

"It wasn't the e-mail."

"How do you know?" He looked at her with skepticism on his face. "You weren't there."

"Have you ever been hypnotized?"

"No."

She could tell by his expression he wasn't open to the idea. "Don't worry, I'm not going to suggest it. I don't even know how to do it."

"But you know what caused my meltdown?"

She nodded. "I want you do something for me." She waited for him to agree.

"All right."

"I want you to close your eyes and return to that day." She moved around, sitting cross-legged on the floor. "You've just come into your office. I want you to tell me everything that happened, everything you did in the order you did it. But I want you to see it, not live it. You're a spectator and you're reporting what you see."

Rose leaned her back against the stair railing. Evan was directly in front of her. "Give me your hands." He put his in hers. She had to adjust her legs to fit in the small space. "Close your eyes."

He did as she instructed. "Okay," he said. "I'm loaded down with stuff as I reach the door. I have my briefcase in one hand, a newspaper under my

arm, a cup of coffee and a bag with two dough-
nuts in it." He opened his eyes. "Not a healthy
breakfast, but I don't eat it every day."

"This is not a session on nutrition. Keep on
track if you want to find out the truth of what
happened."

Closing his eyes again, he returned to the story.
"I put everything on the desk. I'm humming a song,
'By The Time I Get to Phoenix.' It was playing on
the radio when I parked the car in the underground
garage. I turned the computer on. The phone rang."

He dropped Rose's hand to reach for the imaginary phone. His action stopped as if he'd just remembered doing it.

"There was no one there when I picked it up. I
stopped humming. I hung up the phone and took
a drink of my coffee. Then I clicked on the icon to
open the e-mail program, but I swung around in
the chair and looked out the windows. I got up and
went to the windows. The cleaning crew always
pulls the blinds down. Energy conservation. I
pulled them all the way up to let the sunlight in."

"Stop," Rose said. Evan's reaction was to jerk
her hands as if he'd been on a carnival ride that
suddenly stopped. Yet he kept his eyes closed. She
could almost see the movie in his head pause, with
Evan as the only actor, frozen in place. "What
floor is your office on?"

"Second."

"You can hear the sounds of the street."

He nodded.

"Look at the street. Tell me what you see, what you hear."

The pressure on Rose's hands increased. She ignored it.

"It's rush hour. The streets are packed in both directions. Car horns are blowing."

"What else?"

He paused a long while. His brow furrowed. "A siren, two sirens. Fire trucks. I can see them. They can't get through the traffic. The sirens. They keep blaring."

"Don't live it, Evan. Just report." Rose could tell from the pressure on her hands that he'd slipped out of the reporter mode. His grip was so tight he could break the bones in her hands if he didn't relax. "They keep coming. There are more of them, coming from other directions. They get louder and louder. There's no place for the traffic to go. It's totally blocked. The man on the siren won't stop. He keeps blasting the horn."

Rose didn't need a blood pressure cuff to know Evan's pressure was rising.

"It won't stop," he shouted. "It won't stop."

"Open your eyes," Rose said sharply.

Evan's eyes flew open. He stared at her. She'd

snapped him back from his virtual office to the floor in the Maine lighthouse.

"It was the sirens," he stated.

"And the lights. They act as a trigger. What you need to do is not relive the scene when you see or hear one."

"How did you know?"

"Your panic attack the night of Jim's accident. All the symptoms displayed said you had PTSD. And I consulted with Doc Kidd."

"What do I do now?"

"Continue your therapy sessions and try not to relive the event." She released his hands and moved them up his arms in a comforting motion. "You can learn to remember Gabe and Alana without thinking of the fire, without *being* there."

"Is that what you did? After your wedding?"

Rose hoped the jolt that went through her didn't communicate itself to Evan. "Yes," she said. What she didn't tell him was that his appearance in Lighthouse had helped her stop reliving that day. That she had learned that her life would go on. That she still had the capacity to love another man.

And that he was that man.

The calendar in Evan's kitchen told him he was due to leave Lighthouse in a few weeks. He didn't need the reminder. He was as well aware of the dwindling number of days he had left as he was of the shortened hours of daylight. The call from Mike Conroy from his office that morning had been to keep in touch. Mike was a speechwriter and one of his friends. Evan had just come in from his jog when the phone rang. After a few minutes of catching up, Mike had asked Evan when he would be coming back.

The call had Evan thinking about how much he missed the pace of D.C. And how he longed to return but didn't want to cut short his time with Rose. Just before Evan hung up, Mike mentioned that Evan's invitation to the reception for the new ambassadors had arrived. Because Senator DeLong was on the Foreign Affairs Committee she was invited, along with her chosen staff, Evan included. Though it would be good for his career, he told Mike to refuse the invite.

However, he kept thinking of it as he prepared to start his day at the high school.

As Evan ate breakfast he wondered what Rose would say if he invited her to a party—in D.C. He heard her Jeep start up and went to the door. She was at the end of the driveway when she saw him and stopped.

"How would you like to go to a party next weekend?" He didn't give himself time to think about a good way to lead into his invitation. This was Rose and the two of them needed no preamble to their conversations.

"Sure." The smile on her face was big and her eyes danced. "Who's having a party?"

"It's a reception for the newly named ambassadors to the U.S."

Her face fell. "This party is *where?*"

"Washington."

"D.C.? Washington, D.C. Evan, I can't go to Washington."

"Why not?"

"Well, for one thing, I'm the doctor here. What happens if there is an emergency?"

"Doc Kidd is still here. And what happens when the doctor gets sick? Who takes over?"

"Doctors aren't allowed to get sick."

He leaned down to the level of the Jeep's window. "Think about it, Rose. You don't have to answer right away."

"What would I wear? I'm not cosmopolitan, Evan. I'd probably be a country bumpkin in Washington."

"You'd be fine," he told her. He reached inside and pushed a stray strand of hair behind her ear. "You could never be a country bumpkin. Think about it. Give me your answer tonight when you get home."

She looked at him as if she was ready right now to refuse again but changed her mind. "All right.

I'll think about it, but don't hold out that I'll agree."

"I won't." Evan ran his hand down her cheek and across her shoulder before standing up and stepping away from the vehicle. "As incentive for your decision, we can stop by Portland Hospital and see Jim Wiley." Evan didn't feel rejected. He was elated. She was softening. He knew she'd agree. It was a party and he'd dated enough Cinderellas to know that the idea of going to a ball was too much to pass up. Going back in the house, he downed his orange juice in one long gulp and called Mike to let him know he'd changed his mind about the invitation.

And to tell him he was bringing a date.

This was totally unfair, Rose thought. She had considered nothing else all day except Evan's invitation. Going to a formal event, dancing with him under crystal chandeliers in a roomful of people who didn't know her, where she could close her eyes and give full rein to her fantasies—it was too much to ask for.

Should she do it? Doc Kidd had worked alone until she returned last year. It would only be a couple of days. She *could* go.

But *should* she? What kind of signal would that give Evan? He was leaving for good in three weeks. This could be the last time she saw him.

"All right, Rose, what's on your mind?" Filling in for Rose's regular nurse, Brenda was standing in her office doorway.

"Why do you think something is on my mind?"

"Because you haven't been the same since Evan Harper returned to town. Since you got here this morning you've been as nervous as a first-year intern. You're jumpy, disoriented, and you're wearing your hair down."

Involuntarily, Rose's hand went to her hair. "What does my hair have to do with it?"

"I'm sure you know, but I'll tell you anyway. When a woman wears her hair down it makes her face softer, frames her face and accentuates the eyes, making them mysterious and sexy. And that can only mean one thing."

"What thing?"

Brenda put one hand on her ample hip and looked directly at Rose. "That she's on the prowl." Brenda meowed like a cat. "So what has Evan done that has you taking time to make yourself more attractive? And to put that faraway look in your eyes?"

Rose wanted to drop her head, but she held Brenda's wise gaze. "He invited me to a party."

Brenda smiled her approval. Her whole appearance changed. She went from being the stern mother figure to the warm-hearted friend. Coming into the office, she sat in one of the two chairs in front of Rose's desk. "What's wrong with that? It seems natural to the courting ritual."

"I'm not courting him and he's not courting me."

"Honey, you two have danced the third dance."

"What?"

She shook her head, dismissing it. "Ask Evan. He'll explain it to you. Back to the party."

"I'd be too out of place with all those dignitaries," Rose said. "What would I talk to them about, gallbladders or the ritual of Final Day sails?"

"What dignitaries?"

Rose realized she hadn't fully explained. She told Brenda about Evan's early-morning invitation and that she had to answer him tonight.

"So what's the problem?" Brenda asked. "You like Evan. He likes you. You've been to Kings. This is no different."

"It is," Rose contradicted. "First it's in D.C. and second I won't know a soul there. There will be ambassadors from everywhere, not to mention our own government representatives. I'll have nothing in common with them. Nothing to talk about."

Brenda dismissed her concerns. "How did you feel about the Harpers living next door to you?"

"The Harpers?" She didn't understand Brenda's sudden jump in subject.

"Evan's father is the ambassador to Egypt. Did you feel out of place with him and Evan's mother?"

"Of course not."

"Then just assume everyone at the party is like the Harpers."

"You think I should go?" Rose fidgeted with a pencil.

"In a word, yes."

"Brenda, I have nothing to wear to a place like that."

"Portland is only a couple of hours away. You can go there and buy a dress. While you're there you can look in on Jim Wiley. Or you can go to Washington a day early and shop once you get there."

"That's what Evan said."

"He's right."

"I mean about visiting Jim Wiley. He used it as a carrot to force me to accept his invitation."

Brenda laughed. "He's stuck on you." Then she sobered and leaned forward in the chair. She looked directly at Rose. "Is the party the problem or is it going away with him?" Before Rose could answer, Brenda continued, "I assume you two will be staying at his place. Are you afraid he might want more from you than just taking a pretty girl to a party?"

Rose could have answered that many ways, but this was Brenda and she chose to tell her the truth. "I'd be lying if I said the thought hadn't crossed my mind."

"When it crossed your mind—" her voice was soft, girlfriend-to-girlfriend, even though Brenda was old enough to be Rose's mother "—was it with anticipation?"

Rose didn't speak or try to disguise the messages that she'd denied telling herself. That since Evan had returned to the house next door to hers, he was all she could think of. That kissing him had rocked her world. And that the thought of him making love to her had aroused her, body and soul.

Brenda reached over, cupped her chin and looked in her eyes. "I see," she whispered. "It's that bad."

Rose understood her meaning. She had it bad. "Brenda, do you really think I should go?"

"Honey, stop torturing yourself. You want to go. Do what you want to do and stop telling yourself you can't when you can."

"I'll think about it."

And she did. Between each patient she thought of Evan, but not about saying yes or no to his invitation. She thought about being alone with him, away from the small-town mentality of Lighthouse. She thought about seeing his apartment in Washington. And she thought about them making love.

Rose returned to her office after the last patient. She had paperwork that had sat on her desk for days and needed her attention. But her mind was too far away to think about it. Turning to her computer, she opened an e-mail window and sent a message to Mark Carey, head of surgery at Portland Hospital, asking about Jim Wiley's condition.

As she was about to close the program she heard the soft chime indicating she had mail waiting. She thought Mark was fast, but when she looked at the envelope her breath stopped.

It was from Evan.

She laughed out loud when she read it. All it said was *Well?* He didn't even sign it, as if he'd hit the send key by mistake.

Rose replied, also with one word.

Yes.

Chapter 11

"Dr. Albright…Mr. Harper. Who's minding the store?" Despite his obvious pain, Jim Wiley tried humor on them when they came into his hospital room. He was hooked up to a battery of machines. His arms and both legs were encased in casts. Only his fingers and toes were exposed. He had a bandage around his head and was watching television on a set suspended from the ceiling in one corner of the room.

"Doc Kidd told me he was quite capable of maintaining order in Lighthouse while I came to see you."

"Thanks for coming. Being so far from home,

only a few of my friends have been able to get down here."

"How are you doing?" Evan asked.

"I wish I could do something. I can't even lift a book and read." He glanced at his arms. "Not that I was ever a reader, but they don't have cable, and television is a bust."

Evan smiled. "You do look a little like Frankenstein."

Jim laughed and his face immediately spasmed in pain. "Don't make me laugh. It hurts."

"Where do you hurt?" Rose asked.

"The incision." He'd been bleeding internally when the helicopter took him away. She reached for the sheet and pulled it across him to look at the incision, but was stopped by a voice from the doorway.

"I knew you wouldn't be able to resist, Dr. Albright."

"Hi, Doc," Jim greeted him.

Rose turned and found Dr. Mark Carey holding a chart in his hand. He was in his fifties, a man with only a few strands of gray hair, keen eyes and a ready smile.

"Mark." She returned his infectious smile.

"Good to see you again." Rose shook his hand and he kissed her cheek. She introduced Evan. The two men shook hands. "Mark was one of my professors when I was in medical school. He left the university to take the chief of surgery job here a year before I graduated."

"I tried to get her to do her residency here, but she preferred Boston," Mark said with a sardonic smile. "I suppose Portland can't compete with the big city." Then he looked at Rose, who was holding a tight smile.

"Now I need to run you two out so I can examine my patient."

Rose smiled. She'd watched him work and knew he was the best. Jim was in good hands.

"Thanks," she said. She looked at Jim. "See you later, Jim. Sorry we can't stay longer."

"Sure," he said. "Thanks for coming."

Evan leaned close to him and said something in his ear. Jim laughed and again the pain spasm showed on his face. Then she and Evan turned and went toward the door.

"Wait for me outside," Mark told her. "I'd like to talk to you about something before you go."

Rose looked at Evan. He consulted his watch and nodded.

"What did you tell him?" Rose asked as they waited in the hall.

"I told him to have that pretty nurse read to him. And that he should choose a very sexy book."

Rose laughed and punched his arm.

Mark came out moments later. "How is he?" she asked as soon as she saw him.

"Lucky," Mark said. "That fall should have killed him. But he had an excellent GP who knew exactly what to do."

Rose felt her face grow hot with his compliment.

"That's what I want to talk to you about." They had begun to walk toward the nurses' station. "Thought any more about going on and becoming a surgeon?"

She shook her head. "I'm happy in Lighthouse."

For a moment she thought the two men passed a glance between them as if to confirm her words.

"You know Doc Kidd is retiring at the end of year?" she said.

"I'm coming up for his retirement party." He sighed. "But Vernon's retirement shouldn't factor into your decision. Rose, you were born for surgery."

"I'll think about it," she said.

"Which means you won't." He looked at Evan. "Have you got any influence with her?"

"Very little," he answered. "She started bossing me around the moment I got back in town."

"I've had many students and only a few of them have as much natural talent as you." He spoke to

Rose. "And you're hiding it under the mantle of general practitioner. Think of the lives you could save, Rose. You could have been the surgeon saving Jim Wiley's life."

"I said I'd think about it." She spoke more sharply than she'd intended. In a more pleasing voice, she said, "I promise, Mark. I *will* think about it."

"Do you still have the papers I sent you?"

"They're lying on my dining-room table."

"Move them from the table and fill them out."

Evan took her hand as they walked to the elevator after saying goodbye. He seemed to know she needed someone to hang on to.

"*Are* you going to think about it?" Evan asked as they sped along the road toward the airport. "Seems I'm not the only one who knows of your dream of being a surgeon."

"Evan, you know my situation. Could we not talk about this for the next three days? This is the first vacation I've been on since I returned to Lighthouse. Please don't spoil it. I don't want to spend it arguing over what my choices should be."

He gripped her hand. Lightning jolted through her.

"You're right. This is your vacation."

Evan's condo in D.C. was in an pre–World War II building on Connecticut Avenue within walking distance of the White House. The rooms were huge, with high ceilings and large windows. He'd had it decorated in somber colors that were accented with bold artwork. His sofa was a large L-shaped sectional that Rose sank into and never wanted to leave. The living room had a nonworking fireplace, a remnant from prewar days. The dining room was formal with a polished wood table and Chippendale chairs. The open kitchen allowed the cook to interact with his guests.

The fireplace mantel had less depth than any of those in their houses back in Lighthouse, but Evan had pictures of his parents sitting on it. Rose looked around for other pictures. They were the only two in the room. She wondered where the pictures of his son were. And his ex-wife.

Then she realized if he was having problems associated with the child's death, he'd probably been advised to remove them from view.

Evan had put Rose's things in his spare bedroom. They'd arrived in Washington a day earlier than necessary, but not so she could shop. Rose had taken a day off earlier and gone to Portland to find a dress. Instead of Evan contacting old friends or visiting his office, he'd walked her feet off, going to every monument and museum in the capital.

When they returned, Rose plopped down on the sofa, determined not to move ever again.

"I don't know if I'll be able to dance tomorrow," she told him. "With the see-Washington-in-a-day tour you took me on, my feet hurt and my legs are as heavy as logs. The only place we didn't see was the White House."

"I'll make sure you visit it before we leave." Evan came to the sofa with two glasses. Rose expected more cider, but was surprised to find champagne in her glass.

He set his glass on the table and pulled her feet onto his lap.

"What are you doing?" she asked.

"I'm massaging your feet. You have to dance tomorrow."

He removed her tennis shoes and began a gentle massage. Rose lay back and closed her eyes. It felt so good. Her blood boiled and warmed her legs. "You're in the wrong profession," she told him. "You should be in the pleasure-giving field."

"You mean like a male concubine?"

Rose opened her eyes and looked up. She hadn't expected him to say that.

"Of course, that would mean I'd need a harem," he told her. "Would you be part of my harem?" he asked.

She shook her head. "I want a man who is totally and completely mine. I'm not willing to share."

The air in the room suddenly changed. It was no longer just air. It was now filled with sex. Tension. Innuendo. Rose's stomach knotted and her throat went dry.

The air wasn't the only change. Evan's hands moved up her body. Rose wore jeans, but she felt as if her clothes were being burned away. Her skin seared under his touch. He moved closer to her, sliding under her legs as he pulled more of their bodies together. Finally she was sitting in his lap, her arms wrapped around his neck, their eyelashes nearly touching, their mouths separated by a breathless kiss.

"You should kiss me," Rose said.

"Don't worry. I'm going to. But why *should* I?"

"Because you've made this whole day, sore feet and all, one of the best I've ever had."

His laugh was a rumble she felt against her bottom. "Since we stepped off the plane at the airport you've had that Alice in Wonderland look in your eyes. It's like you fell down the rabbit hole."

"I did," she said.

"Is that why you have that Cheshire cat grin on your face?" Evan's hands caressed her side, running up to her breast but not touching it.

Rose poked her bottom lip out in a mock frown. "I thought my smile was a bit wicked."

"Only to my hormones," Evan said.

With their faces so close together, Rose and Evan stared directly into each other's eyes. His comment went through her like lightning pouring through her veins. The tension around them snapped like a live wire. Her heart felt as if it was being squeezed in her chest. Rose read the need in his eyes, the passion and some indefinable depth they both shared.

She leaned into him, removing the infinitesimal space and pressing her mouth to his. His lips were soft. He poked his tongue to the surface, giving her a taste of the pleasure to come. Her legs clinched as her belly began to burn and the fire shot downward.

Evan pulled her to him, rolling on top of her, pressing her breasts to his chest and deepening the kiss. His tongue invaded her mouth, sweeping like a hot flame but leaving behind sensations so delicious Rose didn't want to relinquish it. His hands massaged her back. Tender fingers spanned the curvature, moving to her sides and tempting her breasts as they passed near them. Her nipples tightened in anticipation of Evan's fingers caressing them.

"Do you know how long I've wanted to get you in this position?" Evan asked.

"I have an idea," she said. She wanted to touch him, feel his skin next to hers, ease the weeks of frustration she'd experienced through dreams and the fight to keep him from withdrawing into himself.

She pushed her fingers under his sweater. His body was warm to the touch as her fingers explored his skin.

"Hmm." She made an involuntary sound. Then her hands began to push upward, taking his sweater with them. Evan grabbed the sweater's hem and whisked it over his head. Rose trailed kisses over his shoulders, caressing every inch of him. He felt so good, firm but giving.

His hands tugged at the hem of her blouse, pulling it free of her jeans. He raised his upper body to free the blouse, and she felt his arousal press against her. Rose's eyes closed at the delight that pulsed through her by the simple movement.

As Evan unbuttoned her blouse, his fingers skimmed her flesh as he exposed it, inch by inch.

He pulled her up and nearly tore the blouse down her arms. Then he pulled her back against him, his mouth finding hers, kissing her with a hunger he'd never felt before. Rose reached for the snap on his pants. His hands stopped her.

"The first time I make love to you, I want to do it in a bed," he said. Then he stood up, pulling her with him. He ran his hand through her mussed hair. Rose drank in his warm male scent, thinking that Evan Harper was definitely sexy enough to receive a warning label.

Evan carried her to the bedroom, bright with afternoon light. He set her down on the floor in front of the bed. Both hands pushed her hair over her shoulder and rested on her neck. His thumbs lifted her face and his mouth touched her tenderly.

"If you keep doing this," she whispered, winding her arms around his neck, "my nerve endings are all going to fire at once."

"Will there be an explosion?" Evan nuzzled her neck and Rose found it impossible to speak. She shuddered at the sensations that rioted through her.

"I'm sure there will be." Her voice was a whisper.

"Good," Evan said, and continued driving her wild with his hands and his tongue. She could barely stand.

Evan unsnapped her jeans and, hooking his fingers in the sides, pushed them down to her knees. She raised her feet one at a time and kicked them free.

Rose wore a matching lace demi-bra and panty set she'd bought during her shopping trip to Portland. She'd gone into a lingerie store and come out with a wardrobe she wouldn't dare let her patients know she had on. But she wanted Evan to know. Wanted him to see her this way.

He stepped back and looked at her. "You're beautiful," he said in a husky voice.

"So are you." Rose's words were out before she could stop them.

He gazed at her as he undressed, his eyes never leaving hers. The tension between them was nearly visible.

Stepping forward, she hooked her fingers into his boxer shorts the way he'd done to her jeans. She looked at him with a smile on her face, then slid his shorts down, her fingers splaying over flesh as she went.

Evan drove his hands around her body and released her bra. He slipped the straps down her shoulders and brought the scrap of material around her, taking the weight of her unbound breasts in his hands. Rose moaned when the pads of his thumbs brushed over her sensitive nipples.

She rose up on her toes, her breasts teased by his chest, his hands wickedly working. She deepened the kiss even as she pushed her panties to the floor. She cradled her naked body against his full arousal.

Evan backed her to the bed and joined her on it. She felt the satiny spread beneath her back. From the nightstand he pulled a condom and put it on, then swung his body over hers. Rose anticipated him joining with her, but he held her off. Holding her hands over her head, his mouth closed over her breast, wet and tantalizing. Her nipples grew taut and pointy as if they were reaching for him. Rose fought to free her hands. She had an undeniable need to touch him, but Evan knew it and kept them at bay, making her squirm under him, making her breathless with anticipation.

Finally, he freed her hands while joining their bodies in passionate union. Rose gasped at his entry. A sigh of rapture broke from her. Evan set the speed, and it wasn't long before Rose matched him in intensity, move for move.

"Evan, I'm on fire," she gasped.

Evan didn't speak. He was beyond speech, beyond coherent thought. He grasped her hips and lifted her, thrusting into her deep and hard, until they were speeding so fast the world spun around in a blur. She barely recognized her own voice crying out in reluctance.

Afterward, Evan held her tightly, not wanting to let her go.

Rose held him for a year, a second, a moment, she didn't know. Then Evan slid off her and they lay curled in each other's arms.

Night had fallen when Rose woke. Evan lay sleeping next to her. They'd pulled the spread down and slipped between the sheets. She was still in his arms, surrounded by the warmth of the bedclothes and Evan's body. She snuggled against him, a contented smile on her face.

She didn't know how to define the experience

they'd just shared. Rose didn't know what to expect, but the wild ride they had been on was off the scale for her.

Pushing the covers back, she slipped out of Evan's arms and his bed. Her clothes were strewn all over the house. Finding one of Evan's shirts on a chair, she pulled it on, folding up the sleeves so her hands were free. In the kitchen she poured herself a glass of orange juice and drank it in one long gulp. Refilling the glass, she took it to the living room and went to stand before one of the huge windows that looked out on the busy roadway.

Rose hadn't seen a street this busy since she left Boston. Even the traffic in Portland wasn't this alive. Where were all those people going? Her stomach rumbled. Maybe dinner, she thought. She and Evan had planned to go to dinner before their detour on the sofa had led them to the bedroom and dessert.

She smiled. It was a great dessert. The best she could remember ever having.

A siren came from outside. Evan's condo was on the top floor, yet she could hear it. She looked outside and the fire engine appeared in the window. The cars moved aside and it continued. The Doppler effect rose and fell as it moved farther away from the building. Evan came to her mind in a flash. She turned quickly, staring at the bedroom door. Had he heard it? There was no sound coming from there. Was he still asleep? She took a step, but stopped.

"Over here." Evan stood in the kitchen door. He had a bottle of water in his hand. It was nearly empty. "I heard it." Pushing away from his position, he came toward her. She could see he wore his boxer shorts and nothing else. Her blood pressure and body temperature jumped up several notches. She wondered if this was to be the normal reaction she had to his presence. Everything was new now. Earlier today they had been different people from the ones who now occupied their bodies. Their coming together. Their making love, that journey had taken them light-years from where they began and had returned them to earth as different beings.

"No sweats, no stress, no feelings of panic." He grinned. "At least not the kind I had."

"Are you panicked?"

He put his water down and came to her, bare-hugging her.

Rose had that warm-blanket feel. Not a soft one from the dryer, but one that had worshiped the sun. One that made her feel safe. And loved. She put her arms around Evan's torso. His skin was smooth and smelled of their coupling. She relished the feel of it.

"Am I panicked?" Evan asked. She looked up at him. "Whenever I see you," he said and kissed her.

"Rose, the car will be here in five minutes." She heard Evan call from the living room.

"I'm ready," she said. She slipped her feet into her shoes and surveyed her image in the mirror. For all other purposes, she'd moved from the guest room to Evan's room, but her clothes were still where he'd put them. She dressed in the guest room.

Taking the small, new purse, along with all her other new purchases, she left the room and joined him.

"Wow," she said. A large bouquet of roses sat on the open counter, next to a tray of chocolates and a bucket of chilled champagne.

Evan's back was to her. He turned around and stood stock still. "Wow is right. I thought you said you didn't have anything to wear." She saw the appraisal on his face and knew the dress was worth every penny she'd paid for it.

"I improvised," she said. She looked down at the purple satin gown. It was fitted to her waist, then flowed to the floor in a waterfall of color. The low neckline was square across the front with a V that played peekaboo with her cleavage. The dress had no sleeves but was held up by two straps of rhinestones that glittered in the light. Around her waist was a contrasting wide ribbon of white satin edged with matching rhinestones. It was tied into a bow at her back and the ends fell to the floor.

"That you did."

"When did you do this?" She walked to the counter. Instinctively she cupped the roses in both hands and took in their fragrance. Two champagne flutes sat next to the bouquet.

"I heard that all women like roses and chocolate. The champagne was completely my idea." The ice made a shifting sound as Evan pulled the bottle from the bucket. Using a white towel with all the flair of a wine steward, Evan dried the bottle and poured the golden liquid into the flutes.

"What shall we toast?" Rose asked.

"How about to a wonderful night?"

She nodded, clinked her glass and drank. "Should we be eating candy before going to a fancy party?" She picked up a chocolate-covered cherry and popped it into her mouth. It tasted heavenly.

"This is your appetizer."

"Gee," she said, picking up a second piece that looked as if it contained a pecan. She raised her eyes to Evan. "I've already sampled the dessert. I wonder what the main course is like."

The grin on Evan's face was wicked. "Who

would have thought that little Rosamund Albright could talk so dirty?" He lifted a chocolate square from the silver tray. With slow, deliberate movement he raised it, opened his mouth and placed it on his tongue. Rose swallowed, tasting the sweet richness of the cocoa as it passed out of her mouth and down her throat.

The phone rang. The sound came from far away. Evan remained as he was, as if he didn't hear it. Rose wondered if he could move. She couldn't. Some invisible bond was holding them in place. She looked at the instrument hanging on the wall.

"That better be the limo driver," Evan stated after the third ring, "or we're not going to make this party."

Moments later they were sitting in the back of a shiny black limousine on their way. It wasn't a golden carriage magically transformed from a pumpkin by a fairy godmother, but for Rose it had the same fairy tale–like wonderfulness.

The black car traveled effortlessly through the streets of Washington. Rose watched the buildings sliding by outside the windows. She held Evan's arm, her head on his shoulder, her body curved against his. She was so happy. She couldn't remember ever being this happy before.

Embassy Row was on Massachusetts Avenue, a stretch of several miles with more embassies than any other street in the District. Evan had pointed it out yesterday when he took her on a tour of the city. Yet the limousine crossed Pennsylvania Avenue at Seventeenth Street. Her directions might be off, but she was sure Massachusetts Avenue was in the opposite direction. Rose sat up. She stared through the window, glimpsing the White House a block away. She barely saw the lights before they were out of sight.

She felt Evan chuckling at her.

She punched him. "I've never seen the White House, except in a book or on television."

The driver turned in to a private road flanked by guards who stopped them.

"What's going on?" she asked.

"You said you wanted to see the White House."

The car headed behind the Old Executive Office Building. In the distance was the Washington Monument, imposing in height and grandeur.

She suddenly realized where they were. "You're kidding." Her voice was raspy. She could barely talk. "Can you do this? Is it legal?" The driver turned the car into the semicircle of the porticoed entrance and came to a stop at the doors. A uniformed man opened the door and extended his gloved hand to her.

They got out. Rose and Evan stood on the North Portico, its hanging light above her head, the heavily molded door in front of her. "I thought this was an embassy party. I mean, held at an embassy," she whispered so no one could hear her.

"It's a party for newly appointed ambassadors," Evan whispered back. "It's always held here."

"But this is the White House," Rose said, keeping her voice low. She heard the incredulity in her speech. She couldn't believe she was standing at the entrance door.

"Why did you think you had to go through all those security checks last week?"

"Because it's Washington and there would be so many dignitaries attending. I thought it was standard procedure."

"It is," Evan said. "For anyone entering these doors."

He put his hand on the small of her back and with a slight push her feet remembered how to walk. Passing through the electronic-detection screening and handing her purse over for inspection didn't dull the moment a bit.

"Welcome to the White House," Evan whispered.

Chapter 12

Rose looked over her shoulder as she emerged from the reception line into the main salon. She'd just shaken hands with the president of the United States.

Evan pulled her along, toward the party that was in the East Room. Rose turned her head around and nearly gasped at the elegance of the place; three cut-glass chandeliers, soft white paneling that seemed to reflect the women in sequins and men in evening dress.

"I've seen pictures of this room. They're bad copies compared to this."

"Nothing does it justice except seeing it in person," Evan whispered. "I guess that's why the White House is the most visited house in America."

"Evan, over here." Someone called him. They both turned toward the voice. A forty-something woman with striking red hair, a face with freckles and height of nearly six feet smiled pleasantly at them. She held a champagne flute and was dressed in a strapless gown of royal blue. Her only other adornment was a small pair of pearl teardrop earrings.

"Senator DeLong," Evan said. He extended his hand as he walked toward her to introduce Rose.

"You look well," she said to Evan after greeting Rose and complimenting her gown.

"Never better," he agreed.

"Evan," another voice called and joined the small group on the side of the crowded room. This time it was another senator. Evan introduced her and it appeared a routine had begun. The more people who recognized him, the larger the congregation got. Evan Harper was a very popular person and everyone wanted to shake his hand. After a while Rose had moved back to the edge of the grouping.

"You appear to be losing your escort," someone said near her ear.

She turned to find a man about Evan's age with freshly cut blond hair and eyes the color of brown autumn leaves staring at her.

"He's very popular," she said.

"He is. So while he's ignoring you, why don't we dance."

Rose nodded and allowed him to swing her into the swaying movement of the dance floor.

"You ought to tell me your name before the dance ends," she commented. "I'm not from around here. And I know no one."

"Alexander Chord Winston, lawyer, speech-writer, dancer. Alex to my friends, for which you are now one."

Rose liked the young man. She laughed at his display of flair when he turned her around the floor.

"Rosamund Albright, doctor, friend, two left feet."

"You're doing fine." He glanced down at her feet and back up again. "But you're only a friend. Does that mean the door is open to more *friends?*"

"For whom do you write speeches?" Rose ignored his question.

He looked over his shoulder. "That guy over there."

Rose glanced in the direction he indicated. The president was dancing with the first lady.

"I'm impressed," she said. "I've often thought his speeches are insightful, well thought out and inspiring."

"Thank you. Which one was your favorite?"

"People have favorites?"

"Not really, I just thought I'd ask." They both laughed. "You know Evan will probably be the next presidential speechwriter."

Rose tried to keep her face from changing expression. She only raised one eyebrow. "I didn't know that. I also didn't think Senator DeLong was running in the next election."

"She isn't. Most likely the party nomination will go to Senator Prescott Holmes. He's been campaigning for it since the current office holder took the seat for his second term."

"And this senator wants Evan to be his writer?"

"Are you kidding? He's been trying to steal Evan from Katherine DeLong for years, but Evan is very loyal and he likes her politics."

"Doesn't he like Senator Holmes's politics?"

"He does. But he'll only leave the DeLong camp if he can trade it for the West Wing."

Rose had avoided thinking of Evan leaving Lighthouse. She knew he wasn't staying. He'd told her from the beginning that he was only there for a finite period of time. But somewhere between them painting the lighthouse and sharing kisses that curled her toes, she'd let that one important fact slip her memory. Or she'd pushed it to the back of her mind, unwilling to deal with it. Unfortunately, it wouldn't stay there. And Evan wouldn't remain in Lighthouse.

The song ended and people applauded the musicians. Evan caught her eye and came over. "Sorry," he said. "I didn't mean to lose you."

"Not to worry. She was in good hands," Alex said.

"I hope he wasn't filling your head with his tales."

"He was actually teaching me to dance."

"Thank you, Alex. I'll take it from here." Evan smiled. The music began again and Evan's arms went around her. She smiled at Alex, who gave her a little wave as Evan whisked her away. Rose put her arms on Evan's shoulder and felt as if she'd entered a different world. She forgot about him leaving. This was a vacation for her and she wouldn't let anything spoil it.

"So what were you two really talking about?" Evan asked after a moment. "It couldn't have been your dancing." He whirled her around several times. Rose matched him step for step.

She looked up with a smile. "Loyalty. Politics. Senator DeLong. And Prescott Holmes."

Evan nodded understanding. "He told you about the campaign."

"Which one? The senator's run for the presidency or the campaign he's waging to get you onto his staff?"

"Gee, for the space of one dance, he certainly covered a lot of subjects."

"Are you going to do it?" Rose asked. She kept her breath steady but her heartbeat increased. She wasn't sure what answer she wanted to hear. It was a great opportunity and she knew Evan wanted it.

"If the senator runs and he asks me, I'd jump at the chance."

Rose held her smile, but her heart sank. Evan had only come back into her life a few short weeks ago, yet she'd come to rely on his presence. She felt it being ripped from her. She was going to be alone again when he left. Abandoned to her broken heart.

"It must be very exciting." She groped for something to say. "I suppose your speeches will shape public opinion."

"I believe in him, Rose. I believe the country will benefit with him as president."

"Which one is he?" she asked.

Evan stopped dancing and walked her over to a tall, dark-haired man who definitely looked presidential. Rose recognized him when she saw him.

"Senator Prescott Holmes, meet Dr. Rose Albright. She's the local doctor in my hometown."

He shook her hand. While it wasn't as soft as the president's had been, it was firm and confident. His smile was effective and he looked her straight in the eye.

"It's a pleasure to meet you," he said. "I come from a small town too. We only had three doctors in town. My father was one of them. He got to see just about everything that could come along. I suppose you've seen your share too."

"Lighthouse is probably the same as any small town. I did my residency at Massachusetts General, mainly in trauma, so I was prepared for the multiple types of health needs that could arise."

"I'm sure the town is glad to have you there. Evan told me there was only one doctor in town." The senator glanced at Evan. Then he leaned closer to her and in a conspiratorial whisper said, "He also thinks a lot of you. Maybe I can enlist your aid in persuading him to join my staff?"

"Senator?" An impeccably dressed young man with a no-nonsense face both spoke and appeared at the same time. He whispered something to the senator.

"Please excuse me," Senator Holmes said. "Something has come up. It was a pleasure talking to you." Then he took Rose's hand and squeezed it. He leaned closer to her and whispered, "I'm counting on you."

With a nod to Evan, he left them. Rose noticed a lot of these excuse-me-something-has-come-up conversations were going on. She supposed this was how Washington politics worked. Even receptions were occasions for making deals.

"He's likable, right?" Evan asked.

She nodded. She watched him walking away. He had *it*. That undefinable something that made people listen to him and believe in what he said. Rose was sure she'd vote for him.

"He wants you to join his campaign." It was a statement. "Are you going to?"

"I haven't been asked."

"But you will join him when he does ask?"

Evan didn't get to answer. They were interrupted by Senator DeLong joining them. With her was one of the evening's guests of honor, the ambassador from Ecuador. They needed to speak confidentially. This was communicated nonverbally to Rose. She muttered something about getting a drink. Seeing Alex Winston, she headed for him.

As she reached his side, another man stopped next to him. Rose was nearly speechless. She stopped.

"Dr. Albright, isn't it?"

She nodded, unable to speak, but impressed that with so many people in the room, he remembered her name.

"Would you like to dance?"

Rose remembered what Brenda had told her. *Assume everyone at the party is like the Harpers.* "I would love to dance," she said and was led to the floor by the president of the United States.

If Evan weren't holding Rose in his arms and it wasn't nearly three in the morning, he'd think the night had been a dream. The party was a success in his eyes. Bringing her here was a success. He was with the most beautiful woman at the ball and everyone wanted to know who she was. He introduced her to the senator and the staff. He must have heard "Maine certainly agrees with you," a hundred times. The glances people gave Rose when they commented directed the credit to her.

And rightly so. Evan would put his arm around her waist and hold her close. He felt she deserved it although the reason was different. He let them think it was the power of love. And it was. Rose might have found the trigger for his problem, but without her how long would it have been before he found the real reason for his nightmares? She'd discovered it because she cared about him.

"Did you know I shook hands with the president *and* the first lady?" Rose purred in his ear. She'd had more champagne after they returned to his condo. The bottle they'd left open was now empty and Rose was dancing with him to music playing in her head.

"You danced with him too," Evan said. "The entire assembly, and me, witnessed. You could be on the front page of half the newspapers in the world tomorrow."

She stopped. "Do you think so?"

"It's possible."

She smiled as if the possibility was a truism. "Imagine what the people back home will think." They started dancing again. This time she hummed one of the songs they'd danced to that night. "And all those dignitaries. The colors they wore. Did you see the one with all the medals? I thought he'd impale me when we danced."

Evan led her to the sofa and they sat down. She sat facing him with her back to the chair arm. Her bare feet came up and she bent her knees, clamping her hands around them. "I've been talking about me all night. What about you? Did you have a good time?"

He nodded. "It was more than I expected it to be."

"What does that mean?" Evan had brought the chocolate tray to the coffee table. Rose took a piece and ate it.

"It means I've been to many Washington functions, but this time you were with me." He looked at her seriously. He meant every word. "Are you glad you came now?"

"This has been the most fun I've ever had." She moved forward, crawling to him and planting a kiss on his mouth. Evan pulled her off balance and held her. He deepened the kiss, keeping her with him for a long time.

"You taste like chocolate and champagne," he said.

"Do you like chocolate and champagne?"

"I love it."

"How much?"

"This much." Evan already had his hands around her waist. He pulled her so she lay over his knees and kissed her soundly. Less than twenty-four hours ago they'd made love and repeating the experience had been on his mind since he found her standing before the windows wearing his shirt.

His hands went into her hair, finding and removing every pin she had holding it in place. His mouth rained kisses over her face. He reached for the zipper on her dress and pulled it down. A tremor ran through her when he touched her bare skin.

Her dress fell away, Evan kissed her shoulders, her neck and her breasts, pulling off her strapless bra. His mouth traveled over smooth skin to reach the mounds of her breasts. He caressed them, skimming his teeth over them, taking small nips as if trying to consume her. She arched her back and her body curled around his, almost as if she had no bones but was designed to take his form.

Evan thought he knew what worshiping a woman was like, but holding Rose, kissing her, running his hands over her, taught him a new respect for the word.

She pushed herself back. Her eyes were only half-open, her mouth swollen from his kisses. The warm glow of the light in the room gave her skin a golden tone. Her fingers went for the buttons on his shirt.

"What are you doing?" he asked.

"Preparing you."

He smiled. "I like the sound of that. What am I being prepared for?"

She waited a long moment. The look in her eyes was mischievous, but it quickly changed to a deep and strong desire.

"The best night of your life."

In the morning, Rose refused to open her eyes. She wasn't ready to relinquish the magic that had happened between her and Evan. He slept beside her, his arms around her waist, securing her to him. She turned over, her arms touched his bare chest and she smiled as she kissed his skin, still holding the scent of their lovemaking.

She opened her eyes. The room was bright—it had to be nearly midday. Rose couldn't remember the last time she'd slept this late. Or the last time she'd been this reluctant to get out of bed. All she wanted to do was exactly what she was doing, slide her legs over Evan's, run her hands up his chest and down his arms, feel the silkiness of his skin and bathe in the happiness she felt in his arms.

"Hmm," she heard him say. His eyes didn't open, yet on his face was a grin she'd come to recognize. Last night they had made history. Her statement on the sofa was a bold one. Rose could have told herself the champagne was talking, but from the way she felt about Evan she was prepared to give everything. Make her words true. And she'd proved it. Before they slept Evan had told her it *was* the best night of his life. Contentedly she'd closed her eyes and let sleep carry her away.

"What are you thinking?"

She jumped at Evan's voice, then smiled.

"I was thinking of last night."

"The best night of my life," he said without the slightest trace of insincerity.

"Yeah, that one."

Evan slipped his hand up, supporting his head

as he looked down at her. His face was serious. "It was, you know."

"I know," Rose whispered. Feeling flowed into her, injected like a narcotic, rushing through her system with one of those eye-closing, best-thing-that-ever-happened-to-me sensations.

Evan had pulled her up from the sofa, her dress slithering down her body like a purple waterfall. Like a waltz, they danced around and around, strewing clothing as they undressed each other, coming together as their mutual need grew. While they were still in the living room, Evan covered himself with a condom. He must have known they weren't going to make it to the bed this time.

He lifted her, wrapping her legs around him. Rose gripped his shoulders, enjoying the ride as Even pushed her against the wall and entered her. She nearly screamed at the ecstasy that shocked her system.

Evan's thrusts were hard and fast, and her release left her limp and exhausted. After an aeon he let her slip down the wall.

"This is supposed to be your night," she said, out of breath.

"Oh, it is," he said, leading her into the bedroom. "I'm all yours."

"Promise?" She didn't wait for an answer. She slid out of his arms and down his body, trailing kisses over his chest and back. She felt him tremble and smiled as she continued. His hands reached for her, but she caught them and held them clear. Heat radiated from them, almost lighting the room with its fire. Rose wouldn't let up. This was Evan's night and she intended to make the most of it.

Like a dancer she wove her way around him, her hands playing music on his skin, her body rubbing against his intimately. When he reached for her she stopped him.

"I'm not finished." She licked his nipples one at a time. "Yet." He nearly jumped out of his skin.

"I'm not going to be able to take this much longer," he said.

His body was hard as a rock. She waved her hands over it, barely touching him, prolonging the anticipation. Then she rolled the condom he was wearing off while using the backs of her fingers to tantalize him. He moaned as his head rolled back.

"I thought this was the height of male fantasy," she said.

"It might be, but when the real thing is at hand, fantasy goes out the window." His words were slow in coming and breathy.

Rose stood on her toes, reaching for him. Her breasts tickled his skin. His body pierced into the juncture of her legs. She opened them, adjusting his access. Sighing at the pleasure that went through her, she took in the emotions racking him. She felt the velvety softness and wondered how something could be both soft and hard at the same time.

She kissed his cheek, working her way to the corner of his mouth. He turned to her, seeking her mouth. Rose denied him, moving to the other corner. Evan combed his fingers through her hair and positioned his mouth over hers. Driving his tongue into her mouth, he let loose the pent-up emotions he'd been holding in check since she'd begun this sojourn.

Rose tried to remain in control, but she was rapidly losing it. Backing Evan up to the bed, she pushed him down and covered him with her body. They rolled back and forth across the king-size bed as their mouths sought, searched and found the hotness of the other's need. Rose pulled the drawer open next to the bed and found another condom. Putting the foil wrapper between her teeth she sat back, balancing herself on her legs as she hovered above Evan. She smiled down at him.

"You are bad," he said, his voice thick.

"Yeah," she agreed. She reached up and with deliberate slowness ripped the foil, yanking it along a jagged line until the small circle fell. She caught it before it reached the rippling muscles in Evan's stomach.

"You'd better hurry up with that or we won't need it," Evan said.

As soon as Rose covered him, she sank down on him. Evan reached for her, rubbing his hands over her breasts. Her eyes closed and her head fell back. The eroticism of his fingers was undoing her. She felt as if she had no bones, as if she could bend and stretch in any direction. Evan's hands were hot where they touched her and she craved them. She leaned into him, anticipating his touch and meeting it.

Then suddenly Rose was lost. Something inside her built up and up until she could no longer hold it back. It burst and she was filled with ecstasy, filled with Evan and wanted nothing more than to stay in the paradise they had created.

Being with Evan was like nothing she'd ever experienced. Without trying, they'd ascended to another plane. A place where there was only sensation and passion and rapture. A place where pain was pleasurable and where her screams accompanied climaxes.

The two of them collapsed on the bed. Rose breathed hard, sucking air into her lungs, until her breathing became normal. She hugged Evan, smiling, running her legs over his body. She'd never been so happy—and so scared.

* * *

When Rose opened her eyes the world had changed. Everything about it seemed new and different. She was ensconced in Evan's arms, warm and protected and basking in the glow of newfound emotions. Her body was different too. There was a new craving, a hunger for him—she wanted him to satisfy her again and again. She felt more…alive, more in tune with herself and with Evan. Smiling at thoughts of her wild night with him, she looked up. He was smiling at her.

"Glad you came?" Evan asked.

She stretched out against him, sliding her naked body along his. "Can't you tell?" Rose hardly recognized her own voice. It was teasing and husky. Her body was as bold as it was warm. She had no fear of pressing herself against Evan or feeling him against her. It felt so right, that this was where she belonged.

"I can tell," Evan said. "And I'm glad." He pulled himself up against the pillows, tucking Rose close to him. "I have something to ask you."

She closed her eyes and listened to his heartbeat. It was slightly faster then normal. Knowing she was the cause of the acceleration made her kiss his skin.

"I want you to come here and live with me. I want to marry you."

She froze. Shifting her head, she turned her gaze to him. "What did you say?"

"I said I want to marry you."

Rose pushed herself away from him. She dragged the sheet with her, holding it against her breasts like a barrier to the words she'd just heard.

"I'm in love with you," Evan said earnestly. "Don't tell me everything I've read about the way you feel about me is wrong?"

Rose opened and closed her mouth, but no words came out. Evan touched her arm. "When I first came home, I wanted nothing to do with anyone. I'd had one bad relationship and I wasn't up for another. But you changed all that."

She looked at him, her eyes wide and her throat so tight she thought she was going to cry out.

"You were bossy and made me do things I didn't think I wanted to do. You got under my skin. I found myself waking each day and looking forward to it just because of you."

He took a step closer to her. "Don't you love me, Rose?"

"Evan, I can't marry you." She felt the need to put space between them. She got out of bed, looking for her clothes. Her nakedness suddenly made her feel exposed. Her clothes were in the living room. She went to the closet and grabbed the first thing she put her hand on, a Howard University sweatshirt. She slipped it over her head, its length reaching her knees.

"Why can't you marry me?" Evan got out of bed. Slowly he walked across the room, his nakedness seeming to have no effect on him. His body was perfect, dark brown, athletic, and she knew every solid inch of it. The effect it had on her made her even more nervous. He went into the bathroom and came out wearing a terry-cloth robe.

"I live in Maine. You live here."

"You could move."

"No, I couldn't. I'm the town doctor."

"They'll get another doctor."

"Evan, I wouldn't fit in here."

"You fit well enough last night."

"Last night was a dream. It's not how people live day to day."

"If you stayed here we could make our own life. A day-to-day life."

"Evan, I can't." She sighed. "How would you feel if I asked you to move to Lighthouse?"

"I can't be a speechwriter in Lighthouse. You can be a doctor anywhere," he told her.

"You have a sense of obligation to Senator DeLong. I have an obligation to the town."

"That's not the real reason." His eyes pierced through her. "Is it, Rose?"

She felt a flush wash over her entire body. She stared Evan down, but he won the war.

"The real reason is you like being a martyr."

"A martyr to whom?" Anger flashed through her.

"To yourself. You like being the savior. No one can do it without your hand. You grabbed me the moment I came into town and started organizing my life. Why, Rose?"

She was too angry to answer. This is what he thought of her?

"It's why you won't leave. You're staying there under the pretext that you're indispensable, when the truth is you're hiding."

"You should talk. Didn't you return to Lighthouse so you could hide there?"

"Absolutely," he said. "So I know what I'm talking about. I'm the doctor now. I know all the symptoms." He stopped and took a long breath. "I'm offering you a cure."

"All right, Doctor." She crossed her arms and stared at him. "What am I hiding from?"

"From life. You're inside one of those boxes in your dining room, those boxes you can't open. You say you don't know what to do with them. So they sit there in limbo, waiting for someone to come along and open them, put them in their proper place and use them. But you don't want to do that. You're content to let life exist with the pretense of living. And in Maine you can do it. No one there denies you're needed as a doctor. But you and I know the truth."

Tears gathered in Rose's eyes, but her voice was steady and strong when she spoke. "I apologize for all my shortcomings." She pivoted and left the room, moving into the sunny living area where they'd started their trek to the bedroom. She gathered her clothes in reverse order, snatching them up from the trail they had left. She showered and dressed, packed her bag and was ready to go to the airport when the taxi arrived.

Autumn was in full dress when Evan drove across the Allison Avenue bridge. Rose felt as if she'd been away months instead of only a few days. The trees had turned from green to shades of gold and red and were more brilliant than she could ever remember.

She and Evan had been quiet since their argument this morning. The plane ride had been an ordeal, but two hours in the SUV with a silent statue was as much as she could take.

"Are we going to go through the rest of your stay here in angry silence?" Rose glanced at Evan's profile. His face was hard, set as if he were actually made of the stone she'd accused him of being.

"I'm not angry."

Rose gritted her teeth, gnashing them together so hard the action intensified her headache.

"Well, I am," she shouted.

"What are you angry about? I've told you I love you. I asked you to marry me. So far I haven't heard anything from you other than *I can't*." He imitated her voice.

All of Rose's anger evaporated. "I love you, Evan. I've been in love with you since we were in high school." He moved to take her in his arms. Rose stopped him with her hands on his chest. "It changes nothing," she said. "I'm still the town doctor. And you're still a Washington speechwriter on the brink of getting your dream job. It's just not going to work for us."

She bent her elbows and rested her forehead on his chest. Evan's hands skimmed her arms, then he dragged her closer and settled her against him. Rose wanted to cry, but found she was drained. After a long moment, Evan pushed her back into her seat. They drove the last few blocks in silence. This one more companionable than the previous several hours.

She got out and took her suitcase. Rose wanted to say something. Tell him she'd had a wonderful time. That her life had been forever altered. But there seemed to be no words to explain how she felt. In the end it was Evan who spoke.

"Goodbye, Rose."

Chapter 13

A siren blared as Evan stood looking out his office window at the traffic on Independence Avenue. The fire engine sped through and around the cars then turned left toward the northeast quadrant of the city. He hardly noticed it until it passed and the Doppler sound was receding. The feelings that usually accompanied it didn't come. He didn't shake. His heart didn't accelerate. He didn't think of Gabe or Alana. His thoughts ran where they'd been running since he returned to D.C.

To Rosamund Albright.

He thought when Gabe died that he could never feel as bad as that again. This was a different kind of hurt. It was just as intense. Just as miserable. The same kind of heart-tearing torment that made him want to die.

He'd gone to Lighthouse for a cure, never believing he would actually get one. But Rose had shown him the key that initiated his anguish. Given him control over one circumstance of trauma. But she'd handed him another one in the taking of his heart.

"Evan, do you have those pages ready?"

Evan turned. "What?"

Marissa Goring, one of the other writers, stood holding the doorknob. "The papers? Have you finished them?"

"Just about." Evan hadn't looked at them. He'd been staring through the window for longer than he thought. His concentration was still shot, only this time it wasn't because of the fire. "I'll have them on your desk in a minute."

She nodded, the kind of nod that said she doubted him. That she knew he was lying. Marissa had been doing his job during his absence. Her attitude toward him was cool efficiency.

The rumor mill buzzed more strongly since Evan's return. It had stepped up his association with Senator Holmes. The senator was set to

announce his candidacy for president before
Thanksgiving. Marissa and everyone else was
betting on how soon Evan would tender his resig-
nation from Senator DeLong's staff after the announcement. He knew she was counting on it
being sooner rather than later.

"I know it's only been a week since you've
come back. If you want I can finish it up."

"I'm almost done," he lied. "I'll get it to you
in a moment."

She stared at him for a long moment. Evan
could tell there was more she wanted to say, but
she closed the door and left him alone.

He went to the pages on his computer screen.
Pushing thoughts of Rose aside was a monumen-
tal task, but he did it for a while and concentrated
on the speech. It was close to an hour before he
shipped the file over to Marissa's e-mail account.
As soon as he hit the send button the envelope
signal appeared telling him he had an incoming
message on his personal e-mail account.

His breath caught.

Evan blinked, making sure his eyes were seeing
the configuration of letters as they were and not
only as he wanted them to be.

He had a message from Rose. As he reached to
select it, his hand shook. He wondered what was
wrong with him. He hadn't been this afraid since

he was in seventh grade and wanted to ask Jinny Blake to his first nighttime school dance.

Dear Evan,
We left so much unsaid that last day. I can't put into words

It ended in the middle of a sentence, as if she'd hit the send button by mistake. Quickly, Evan checked for another message from her, but there were none. She had obviously made a mistake.

Evan read the note three times. Then he read it again. What can't she put into words? He searched for meaning in the scant collection of words. Was she changing her mind? They'd both had time to think. Time to understand how life would be without the other.

For him it was miserable.

Was it that way for her too? He waited all day for another message. For the completion of the one she'd left open-ended. None came. He wanted to write back. He started several messages but trashed them all. It was Rose who needed to decide. As much as Evan wanted to reach out to her, he couldn't. The next move had to come from her.

By the time he got home, he'd still had no further messages from Rose. Evan rambled around his condo, restless. Standing at the refrigerator, he found himself holding the door open with no recollection of what he was looking for. He closed it and went to the window.

He hadn't slept well since he'd come back. People were beginning to notice, once again asking him if he was all right. He wasn't. And not likely to ever be again, without Rose. Yet she was also here. He could still smell her perfume, hear her voice. At night he'd reach for her in bed and wake up with empty arms.

Damn! Evan cursed to himself. He'd worked hard to get where he was. And what he wanted was within reach. The call had come late today, before he left the office. Senator Holmes wanted to talk to him. He was only a step away from being tapped for the White House.

Why had he thought going home was a good idea? Why did he think getting closer to Rose would lead him anywhere, but where he was right now? He couldn't go back and change the past. He knew he wouldn't want to if he could.

Staring at the evening sky, Evan knew he couldn't go on like this. He'd had a taste of what hiding his feelings had done to him.

Reaching for the phone, he picked up the receiver. It was time to call Senator Holmes.

At home, Rose roamed from room to room. She'd been doing it for hours, ever since she'd mistakenly sent that message to Evan. She wanted to explain things, try to repair the rift in their friendship. Bereft that they'd moved past friends to lovers left her alone and lonely. Now there was nothing between them. Not even the friendship they had shared for most of their lives. In the end she couldn't send the message, couldn't even finish it. She had so much to say and nothing came, nothing that made any sense. Then ironically she'd hit the wrong key when she was signing off. The message was gone. Sent. She stared at the computer screen shouting for it to come back. But it was no use. That mistake made her more depressed than she already was.

And Evan hadn't responded.

Maybe he hadn't received it yet, she thought. Surely he had an office e-mail account that he monitored several times a day. What would he think when he got her truncated message?

Selecting a bottle of water from the refrigerator, Rose switched on the kitchen television. Maybe the noise would quiet the scenarios running through her head. Scenarios on how she could explain the message. How she could rationalize it to herself and to Evan, if he replied.

None of them presented anything that would work. She pulled out a chair and plopped down on it, propping her feet on another one. Moving from channel to channel, she searched for something to occupy her mind. After twenty minutes of surfing, she stopped on a news station and listened for a few minutes. When that didn't help, she decided to go to her office and finish some paperwork she had waiting. Picking up the unopened bottle of water, she returned it to the refrigerator.

Reaching for the remote control to turn the unit off, a photo embedded in the corner of the screen stopped her action. She listened to the commentator. "...Senator Prescott Holmes, who was expected to throw his hat in the presidential ring after Thanksgiving, made the announcement last night at a press club dinner..."

The anchorwoman continued speaking, but Rose no longer heard what she was saying. It was done now. The senator was a candidate and Evan would join his staff. Rose stared at the screen, her body completely numb. She didn't know what to feel. Evan was achieving his life's dream. Her message no longer mattered. Any chance for their relationship had just been buried.

Crossing the floor in two easy strides, Rose smacked the power button to silence the report. She had to get out of the house. Suddenly the room was too claustrophobic. She turned and headed down the hall. Her parka hung on a coat tree near the door. Determined steps hit the hardwood flooring in rapid cadence. As she passed the pocket doors to the dining room, she skidded to a stop. For a moment she stared at the panel doors. Grasping the two finger pulls, she yanked them apart. They flew into the recessed walls with a bang.

Stepping inside, she snapped on the overhead lights. The boxes sat accusingly as she'd left them. She reached for the first one and read the side of the box. A toaster. Like they didn't already have one. She threw the box behind her. It landed with a thud as she went to the second box. A set of knives. They followed the toaster. Bedsheets, pots and pans, a coffeemaker, wineglasses, cheese boards, three of them, settled into a heap on the floor.

As Rose finished the boxes on the table, she started in on those sitting on the floor. Halfway through the pile she opened a set of china. Service for twelve. Rose felt like taking each plate out and throwing them against the wall, but they were from her parents. The anger left her.

Sitting back on her heels, she sighed and looked at the chaos she'd created; pink, silver, a mountain of boxes, some open with their contents spilling out. She grabbed the last box, an unopened wedding gift. There was a card. Rose threw it toward the pile. It was well past the polite time to send thank-you notes. Tearing the paper away, she found matching jewelry boxes inside. His and hers. The beauty of the carved wood caught her breath. She could smell the newness of the wood. The hand-polished stain perfectly matched the bedroom furniture she and Brett had chosen.

The cases were hand-made and beautifully carved. Rose was in awe over them. She opened hers. The inside was covered with navy blue velvet. In one of the drawers was a gold bracelet with her name on it. Who gave them these? she wondered.

Combing through the pile of debris, she searched for the carelessly tossed card.

"Oh my," she whispered when she found it and tore it open. They were from Brett. He'd made them himself. Why hadn't he told her? She was sure they hadn't been in the apartment when they'd opened the other gifts. He must have snuck them into the apartment. Tears misted in her eyes. She wiped them away with her fingertips. Picking up the bracelet, she found a second inscription inside the circle.

Rose held it close to her face. "Remember," was all it said. But Rose understood it. He was reminding her of their agreement that she go on after his death.

Rose stood up, holding the bracelet. She looked

over the dining room, from the wedding gifts to the computer equipment strewn over the window seat and floor at the other end of the room. She moved to the table and opened the last bank statement that had arrived from Security Bank in Boston. This was Brett's legacy. So much of him was embodied in inanimate objects. The remnants of an entire person's life sat in this room. She looked down at the statement. An idea came to her. She would remember and she would go on. But first she had to deal with a bank in Boston.

With the papers still in her hand, she returned to the kitchen and picked up the phone. She'd opened the wedding gifts. Some of them she would use. Others she'd donate to the church rummage sale. Helen Talbott could use the computers for her nursery school. Rose smiled and for the first time in a long while she felt as if she was going to be all right.

"Thank you all for changing your schedules and accepting this meeting." Rose stood up and gathered the hand-drawn designs, budget projections and bank statements in front of her. Doc Kidd stood next to her. The three members of the town council on the other side of the conference table got up with approving smiles on their faces. In turn they each shook her hand, then Doc's.

While the meeting hadn't changed Rose's opinion regarding voting for Jeff Altman, Hank Becker and Doris Sorensen had shown her they were both intelligent and interested in the welfare of the town.

"Are you sure you want to go through with this?" Doc Kidd asked. "As we said, the committee has been working to get more doctors to practice here. We're getting close." Doc Kidd was on the committee to hire more doctors for the township.

"I'm sure," Rose said, putting the papers in a flat leather pouch. "It's what I want and I'm sure Brett would have agreed with me."

She and Doc left the conference room at Town Hall. When they emerged from the building, the air was cold and the wind strong. Rose felt as if it had just blown a heavy weight from her shoulders. Adventure faced her and it was exciting. She was going to study to be a surgeon, and she was leaving Lighthouse in good hands. She and Doc Kidd had proposed a clinic and more doctors for the town. The council had jumped on the idea. Using the money Brett left her to build a clinic seemed like a wonderful idea. One she knew Brett would have loved.

"How about we go to Maxwell's and get a bite to eat?" Doc suggested.

"I need to go back to the office." Rose wasn't very hungry lately and she was reluctant to go home, reluctant to see anything in Lighthouse. Even the revolving light reminded her of Evan.

"Patients waiting?" he asked with raised eyebrows.

"I canceled today's appointments. I didn't know how long this meeting would last. I have some paperwork to complete."

"Good, papers'll be there tomorrow." Doc dismissed her plans. "Let me buy you a cup of coffee."

Rose hesitated a moment, then went to the stairs. Doc Kidd's tone told her she was in for a lecture whether she wanted it or not. He'd been her mentor in the past and his comments had always helped her.

Town Hall sat at one end of Main Street, the Medical Arts Building at the other. Maxwell's café was equidistant between them. They walked, pushed by the wind at their backs. Rose stepped inside, glad to be out of the wind. She avoided looking at the booth where she and Evan had sat. Taking a seat at a table next to the windows, Doc Kidd dropped into the chair across from her.

"Two coffees and two slices of apple pie," he ordered for the both of them when the waitress came over. Rose thought that a bit strange, but she didn't argue. She wasn't hungry.

"How's the packing coming along?" she

asked, delaying whatever he'd been waiting for her to discuss.

"I've got everything boxed, labeled and ready to go. I didn't tell you in the meeting, but I'll be leaving in a couple of weeks."

"What?" She was taken aback. "I thought you weren't going until January."

"That was the plan, but the buyer I had, the one I told you about when you came by that day."

Rose nodded. It was the day she'd confirmed Evan's PTSD.

"Deal fell through," Doc said.

"I'm so sorry, Doc." She frowned, knowing he really wanted to get things settled by year end.

He waved his hand, dismissing her sympathy. "Another one came along. Rather quickly, too." Doc grunted a laugh. "I guess Matilda wanted her commission to buy holiday gifts." He referred to Matilda Philben, Lighthouse's only real estate agent. "New owners taking possession the end of the month. Be leaving a week from Friday."

"So soon, Doc?"

"Had to move fast. Good thing I was already packed. My daughter's excited. She's getting everything ready for Thanksgiving. I can't wait to see the grandkids. I'll be staying with them till my place is ready in January."

Rose knew it was hard leaving family and friends behind. She hated to see Doc go, but his daughter and grandchildren would be glad to have him with them for the holidays. She would miss him. Last year she'd had dinner with him and a few neighbors on Thanksgiving. This year she wasn't sure what would happen.

Evan jumped into her mind. Thoughts of him were never far from the surface. For so many years while they lived next door to each other, their families had intertwined on holidays. She'd thought the two of them would continue that tradition this season. But he'd left the day after they'd returned from Washington.

She knew it the moment she got up the next morning and found his car missing from the driveway. The white rocking chairs had been removed and the house had an empty look about it.

He'd said goodbye to her at her door. She knew it was final, but she hadn't expected he would be gone so suddenly. Before his defined three months came to an end.

"I know you're thinking about what we just did at the council meeting."

Doc's voice brought her back to the table.

"Don't get me wrong, Rose. It's a wonderful thing you're doing. This town needs a hospital. I should have been in those council meetings years ago, forcing them to confront the situation instead of just talking about it."

It was more a clinic than a hospital, Rose thought. A ten-bed facility that could handle some emergencies. There would be two birthing rooms and an operating facility. They would be able to house patients who needed care but weren't sick enough to be flown to Portland.

"It's a start," Doc told her. "If you hadn't come and asked me to be part of it, I'd have left you alone here. I'd have felt guilty about it, but there was nothing more I could do. The council should have done something long ago. I should have insisted."

"Doc, you were alone," Rose said. "How could you be the only doctor in town and attend council meetings too? At least I've had you."

Rose thought about the meeting they'd just come from. She'd been up most of the night preparing her presentation. After she'd gotten over the urge to destroy the boxes in her dining room, she'd gone over the bank statements. Brett had left her a small fortune. If she invested it wisely she could live on it for the rest of her life. But Rose didn't need the money. She had a good practice, and her grandmother had named her as the sole beneficiary in her will.

She used some of her inheritance to pay for

college and medical school. The rest she'd invested. Brett's legacy was larger than she'd thought. And with the council's budget, it was enough to start.

Early this morning, Rose had gone to Doc's and outlined her plan to build a hospital in Lighthouse and get more doctors on staff. Doc had jumped in with both feet, asking to be a second investor. He said he had sizable investments. There was nothing to spend the money on in Lighthouse and he had more than enough to live on. So they'd gone over her plan and budget, redeveloping it in places. Doc knew a lot about the cost of equipment and materials. After that he'd called the council for a meeting.

"The hospital aside," Doc said. "I didn't ask you here to talk about building it or to tell you about my leaving," Doc Kidd said after their coffee and pie arrived.

Rose knew that. "Is there something you need to consult with me about?" Rose drank from her cup.

He sat up straighter. "Yes," Doc said. "I have a patient I want to talk about."

"Who is it?"

"You."

"Me?" She sat the cup back in its saucer.

"Yes, you. I'm leaving and I need to know that you're going to be all right."

"Of course I'm going to be all right." Rose smiled her brightest smile. "I have this hospital to build. You'll be back consulting and here at least four times a year to help out and check on things. You can check on me too."

"You're not all right now," he said. "You're unhappy and you're not eating. If you're going to be here for your patients, you have to be here totally."

"I understand, Doc," she told him.

"Do you?" he asked. "I know you think Lighthouse won't survive without you, but it will."

"Doc, how can you say that? For years you were the only doctor in town. Now that you're leaving, the town will again be down to one doctor and no hospital."

"So you're going to throw away your chance at happiness to take care of the town? You've given yourself another project, one that can totally consume you."

"I am not."

"Rose, the council can do the hiring of an architect, approve a plan, hire a builder. They can hire consultants to screen doctors."

"Well, I can't leave it up to Jeff Altman. Look how much he's accomplished since he's been on the council," she said sarcastically. Jeff had been on the council for as long as Rose could vote.

Doc chuckled. "You got me there." He sobered and leaned forward. "If you don't like that idea you can turn the project over to a group of consultants. They can find and screen doctors. You can oversee the decisions, but you don't have to take responsibility for all the details. All I'm saying is give yourself some time for you and stop hiding here."

"I am not. I—"

Doc raised a hand to stop her.

"You had some bad luck in Boston. And you hightailed it back here and hid in that house." He raised his arm and pointed in the direction of her house.

"Doc, I'm out every day." She could hear Evan echoed in Doc's words.

"You go through the motions of having friends, but you're always on the edges, watching other people live, not doing it yourself. With Evan being here, you came close. I thought you were finally emerging from the shell you're encased in, but he's gone and you're back in hibernation."

Rose swallowed. She had tears in her throat and wouldn't say anything until she was sure she could do it in her normal voice.

"Doc, you spent your whole life here. What would happen to all these people if I moved away?"

"Before I answer that, tell me—do you love him?"

Rose looked down at her untouched wedge of pie. "More than I want to take my next breath."

"Does he love you?"

"Yes," she said. Evan had said he loved her. Rose could hear his voice in her head as he said it, like it was the most important thing on earth.

"Then go to him, Rose."

"I can't." She looked around the café. "See Harry over there? I set his kid's leg when he broke it ice skating last year. The waitress, Abby, her baby was breach. What would have happened to her if there was no doctor in Lighthouse? And—"

"I get the picture," he said, stopping her from continuing. Every person in that room had been to see one or the other of them or had a family member they had taken care of.

"Now with building this hospital and hiring staff, I'm going to be busier than ever."

"It's another crutch, Rose. Another reason for you to put your life on hold. Something else to hide behind."

Rose's shoulders dropped. She didn't want to face the truth. But there it was. Doc Kidd knew it. Evan knew it too. "Doc, Evan left without a word. You don't do that to someone you love."

Doc ate a healthy bite of pie and took a gulp of coffee. "I'm sure it wasn't that cut-and-dried."

Rose closed her eyes and opened them again. "Evan has a whole life ahead of him. He can't come here and I can't go there."

"Why not?"

He said it so matter-of-factly that Rose was taken aback. "We just left a meeting where we're going to build a hospital. You're leaving in two weeks. I have to take care of the town, the plant, and oversee construction."

"It's a lot, isn't it?"

"Of course it is."

"And you can't think of a solution to work it out?"

"Doc, I know you look at me like a father, and I consider myself one of your daughters too, but I don't know why you're driving this point so hard."

"For that very reason. I don't want you to spend your life here and have nothing to show for it when you get to be my age but the fact that you sacrificed everything for the town."

After his statement, the diner was as quiet as a clear midnight on a Sunday. People talked, but Rose and Doc were suddenly enclosed in a bubble that excluded everyone except the two of them. She never realized Doc had sacrificed so much.

"Of course, I married and I had children, but I was a prisoner here and you're about to follow in my footsteps. I don't want that to happen."

Rose was at a loss for words. She looked at Doc

and spread her hand. "What is the solution? Are you suggesting I chuck it all and go running off to D.C.?"

"I don't know. That's for you and Evan Harper to work out. But I'll tell you this. There is a solution. You just have to find it."

The wind batted Rose's back, but she did little more than pull her coat collar up against it. The trees rustled like a hundred voices whispering in a room and the river gurgled over the giant rocks they'd played on as children. Rose watched the black water below the Allison Avenue bridge. She couldn't see it in the moonless night, but she knew it was there.

In her hand she held the silver baby rattle. Evan had given it to her. He no longer needed it as a crutch. She now used it as a talisman, hoping it could work magic and bring him back to Lighthouse. It had worked magic in reverse. She didn't think Doc Kidd would be the magician, but he'd given her the key. Rose rubbed an imaginary spot on the rattle. She smiled. Even though the rattle represented tragedy for Evan, it made her feel closer to him. But it didn't help with her decision.

It should be easy. She loved Evan and he'd said he loved her. She believed him. Yet leaving Lighthouse brought back thoughts of Brett and her tragedy with him. She'd come home after his funeral, back to safety, back to the comfort of home. If she went to Washington, if she married Evan, it could all happen again. Could she take that kind of hurt again?

Rose stood there a long time, her arms leaning on the rusted metal. She could almost feel Evan's arms around her. She closed her eyes and imagined them together. Suddenly there was no wind. She was warm, enveloped in a calm eye that had none of the forces of nature or laws of physics to keep her on the ground. She didn't know how long she existed on this plane, but it was a wonderful place. She felt Evan's love, and her own love for him. Emotions crowded in on her like returning family. She never wanted to leave this place.

But she was going to, at least temporarily. Her suitcases were in the car and she was headed for Portland airport. She'd stopped on the bridge because it reminded her of Evan and she didn't know what would happen once she crossed it entirely and began an adventure that could end in more heartbreak.

The blare of headlights jarred her. Jerking toward them, she squinted and closed her eyes at the sudden pain of the surprising light. At the same time the rattle she'd been holding slipped from her hands. Shifting back with the swiftness of a ballet pirouette, Rose lunged for the small object. Her hand nearly reached it, but it fell. She heard the soft clatter of metal on metal accompanied by the shifting of the beads insides the toy.

Rose saw it poised on the small offshoot a few feet below her. Leaning over, she reached for it. Her hand stretched, but she needed several more inches to grab it. Holding on to the metal brace, she hefted herself up and leaned farther.

Still her hand was inches away from the rattle. Balancing on one foot and holding the railing with all her strength, she groped for the baby's toy. Just as she had it in her grasp, strong hands grabbed her waist and hauled her backward over the safety rail.

"What the hell are you doing?" an angry voice shouted at her. Hands spun her around to face an equally angry man.

"Evan!" she shouted.

Chapter 14

Evan's heart thundered in his chest. When he turned the woman around and confirmed that it was Rose, he pulled her so tightly to his chest, he cut off her breathing. She'd been on the bridge. Evan had never felt this angry and this much in love at the same time.

"What are you doing on the bridge?" he asked.

"I dropped something."

"And it was worth your life to try and get it?"

"Evan, I wasn't trying to kill myself. I wanted to get…"

"What?"

She opened her hand and let him see the small rattle lying in the middle of her palm. "I dropped it," she whispered. "I was trying to pick it up before it fell in the water."

"Don't ever, *ever*—" he pulled her close, holding her to him, burying his face in her hair "—do that to me again. I thought I was going to die when I saw you going over the railing."

Rose kissed his cheek and rested her head on his chest. "I'm so glad to see you. When I woke up the morning we came back from D.C. and found you'd left, I thought I'd go out of my mind."

"I did go out of my mind. I can't live without you in my life. So I'm coming back to Lighthouse."

Rose pushed herself out of his arms and stared at him as if he'd lost his mind. "You're what?"

"I chucked my job. All I have to offer you is an unemployed speech writer. I can't be a speech writer here, but I can be a lawyer or a teacher if there are any openings left."

"You did that?" Her breath was nearly gone. "You quit your job?"

"Resigned yesterday. I want you, Rose. Nothing else matters. Not the job, not working in the White House. If you're not with me, it means nothing."

Tears rolled down Rose's face. Evan lifted her chin and looked into her eyes. "I love you," he said. "I want you to be my wife."

"Evan, I can't let you do that for me."

"It's done," he told her.

"Then we have to undo it. I know how much working in the White House means to you. I can't, won't, let you give up your career, your *dream,* for me."

"There is no other way," he said. "You value the people of Lighthouse enough to make them your priority. I value you as much."

"You'd never be happy as a high-school teacher. Not for the long run. Not knowing what you gave away. Not for the length of a marriage."

"As long as I have you, I can stand it," he said.

For a long moment the two of them stared into each other's eyes. Rose moved away from him. She walked along the bridge then turned back. The lights of his SUV eclipsed her figure over his body.

"I don't want you to stand it. I want you to love it," Rose said.

"I will, Rose. I love you and I'll love whatever I do as long as you're with me. What do you say? Will you marry me?" Evan held his breath.

"I love you, Evan," she started.

"And?"

"And I'll marry you." She could see the smile on his face as he started toward her and raised her hand. "I'll marry you if you go for what you want."

"Rose, you're what I want."

"But I also want you to be who you are. You pointed it out to me. You were right. I have been hiding here." She spread her hands, encompassing the town. "I used Lighthouse as my sanctuary, afraid of the world, afraid of going for what I really wanted. Afraid of being hurt. But I can't shut it out. You showed me that. I love you and I want to be with you. I want to be happy."

"But we can't have it both ways."

She came to him then. "We can have it all," she said. In the cold, windy morning on the Allison Avenue bridge, Rose shivered.

"You're cold, let's get in the car." Evan took her arm and turned her toward the SUV. He stopped at they passed her Jeep. "Is that a suitcase? Were you going somewhere?"

She nodded. "I was coming to you."

He hugged her closer and walked her to the warm cab of his SUV. They sat in the back seat. "Tell me everything."

She explained about Brett's accounts, her and Doc's investments, the council meeting, the details of building a hospital and hiring more doctors. About her talk with Doc in Maxwell's restaurant. And finally her being on the bridge with her suitcase in the Jeep.

"So how are we going to have it all?" Evan asked.

"You take the job with Senator Holmes. I'll build the hospital and hire the new doctors. You'll be away a lot. So will I. We get married at the end of the campaign. By then there will be more doctors here and I can return to school to study surgery. It's my dream. I can't do that in Lighthouse. But I can do it in Washington."

"This is more than I could have hoped for," Evan stated. "There's only one flaw in the plan."

"What's that?" Rose frowned.

"I will not wait a year to dance the third dance."

"The third dance?"

"Don't worry about it. I'll explain it on our wedding night." Evan took her in his arms and kissed her passionately. Rose finally had everything—her friend, her lover and her future.

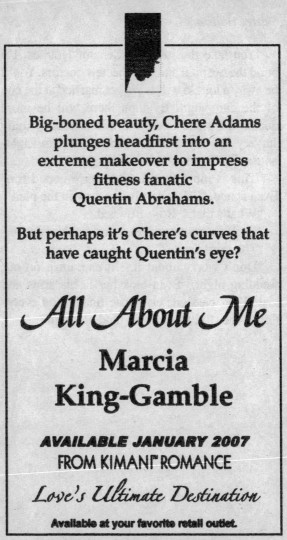

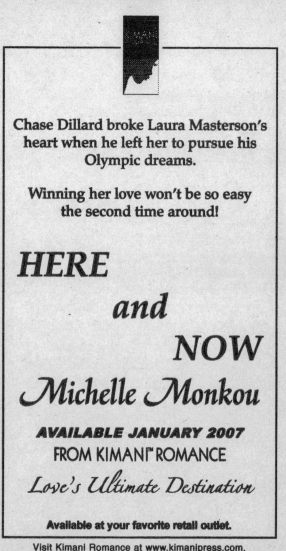